D1033965

THE SOUL OF MALAYA

Henri Fauconnier

THE SOUL OF MALAYA

BY

HENRI FAUCONNIER

TRANSLATED BY

ERIC SUTTON

KUALA LUMPUR
OXFORD UNIVERSITY PRESS
1965

Oxford University Press, Ely House, London W. 1

GLASGOW NEW YORK TORONTO MELBOURNE WELLINGTON

BOMBAY CALCUTTA MADRAS KARACHI LAHORE DACCA

CAPE TOWN SALISBURY NAIROBI IBADAN

KUALA LUMPUR HONG KONG

English translation first published in 1931
by Elkin Matthews and Marrot
This edition published by arrangement with
George Allen and Unwin Ltd.

Photographically reprinted from sheets of the first edition
by Akatsuki Art Printing Co., Ltd. Tokyo

CONTENTS

PUBLISHER'S FOREWORD

When the East Asian Branch of Oxford University Press first considered reprinting this classic work—winner of the Prix Goncourt in 1930—they wrote to the author in the hope that he might be willing to contribute a valedictory preface to the Malayan scenes he knew so well.

Pleading age and illness, he replied regretfully that he was unable to do so, but sent instead an article written during the war, in which he recorded the changes in a planter's life since the days when he himself was one.

The following translated extracts make it plain that he has lost none of his evocative powers of writing, nor any of his memories of Malaya as it used to be:

Even recently, there was in France complete ignorance as to what a planter was. I still remember the short silence which greeted this word, when someone asked me about my job. Astonishment was hidden, no one wanted to appear to be taken in, the joke was politely smiled at, and when it had to be finally admitted that I really was a planter, agreement was distant, and then the conversation was quickly and kindly changed in order not to humiliate me, and also to avoid a recital of the misfortunes I must have undergone before arriving at such a point....

Times have changed.... The French people have studied geography, and they know that the world is a vast and frightening place, and they are grateful to those who engage in the constant search for raw materials.

For the planter, also, times have changed.... Between the Malaya of my youth, and the Malaya of today there is as much difference as between Gaul before the Roman conquest and France as we know it. In twenty years I have seen this country make good a delay of twenty centuries.

There was the age of the little hut. To find land suitable for cultivation, the planter had to cross the coastal marshes, follow mysterious water courses, drive into the heart of the virgin jungle, and open up a road through the lianas, the bamboos and the undergrowth. The site once chosen, a small portion of the jungle was felled and fired. The planter lived in a hut made of bamboo and palm leaves on the edge of the burnt-out clearing, which little by little spread out around him, leaving him in the middle of a black and desolate desert. He had no furniture, the bare minimum of clothing, and lived on rice and tinned foods. The destruction of the jungle, and the flight of the animals who had lived there, created an austere solitude. The great events of his life were the appearance of the first growth in his nursery of rubber seedlings—two little green leaves announcing that life was at last being renewed in the midst of desolation—an encounter with a wild beast or a troop of elephants in the course of his exploration of the jungle, an attack of fever, or a letter from Europe arriving rolled up in the pleats of a Malay *sarong*. He lived all day among his coolies, learning their language and their customs, incorporating the functions of king, judge, and doctor, self-reliant in his loneliness, all-powerful, and abandoned.

Then came the age of the wooden house. Other plantations were opened up all around, and roads traversed the jungle. Bordering the road appeared a Chinese shop where it was possible to procure tea, coffee, cigarettes—and better still, fresh bread. Passing ox-carts were to be seen, carrying furniture from the town, frozen Australian meat, acetylene lamps and bicycles. The plantation stretched out into the distance, its rows of trees bright green against the red earth. Tapping began, and a factory was put up. The price of rubber rose month by month, and every steamer unloaded at the ports a quota of business men from London, Brussels and Paris, suddenly curious to see these, hitherto unknown countries, now revealing such a rich future. Capital was plentiful.

Several years later, we come to the age of stone and cement. The planters are now working for powerful companies who lodge them in bungalows and provide every comfort. Electric light comes from the factory, from which one can hear day and night a constant slow pulsation. Cars rumble down the roads. The coolies ride to the Chinese shop in a taxi. The planters have their central club where they meet in the evening to discuss the latest methods of cultivation, seed selection or grafting seedlings. Life is less difficult, less dangerous, but it is complicated by new worries and heavier responsibilities. The old-time planter, and the planter of today come from the same stock, but circumstances have created different types. If comparing them one could say that the first had been a young man ready to take all risks, the other is a mature man concerned with avoiding risks: the primitive man of action, compared with the civilized reflective thinker, because with security comes worry. It is no easier to conserve and improve than to create. To be a simple planter is no longer enough, it is now necessary to be an administrator, an accountant and a scientist. Everything depends on your intelligence and tenacity, and if it is true that you are now only a cog in a big machine, you are a precious, vital, cog.

His own letter to us closes with these words '...mais je veux vous dire combien je suis heureux de savoir que ma chère Malaisie se souvient encore de moi et me fait l'honneur de rééditer mon livre'.

FOREWORD TO THE ENGLISH EDITION

In offering this book to the English-speaking public, may I remove a possible misconception. I am aware that the beau rôle *is given here to my two Frenchmen, but this was inevitable, as they are the main characters in the narrative as well as my spokesmen. Moreover, my object being to give an insight into the* soul *of Malaya, this could only be attained through the medium of rather exceptional individuals. It follows that my Frenchmen are not ordinary Frenchmen (nor, I must admit, representative planters), whereas the Englishmen who appear incidentally through the book had to be chosen amongst the crowd of ordinary, typical colonists whom one may meet anywhere within the Tropics. My somewhat sophisticated Frenchmen are my heroes in fiction, but their hearty, bluff English comrades were my friends in life.*

H. FAUCONNIER

Radès (Tunisia), September 1931.

I

PLANTER

I

PLANTER

> Jikalau tidak Karna bintang
> masakan bulan terbit tinggi
>
> Jikalau tidak karna abang
> masakan datang adek k-mari

I

THE anniversary of the armistice was celebrated in Kuala Paya by two minutes' silence and two days' orgie. But the orgie of the second day, which was a Sunday, confined itself respectably to the club and to the homes of the little Japanese girls who pretend to invite you in for tea, and only sober cases of drunkenness were met with in the streets.

I shall never forget those two solemn minutes on the Saturday morning: then it was I saw him—the man I had been looking for and never hoped to meet again. He appeared on the veranda of the club where the British Resident, the officials, and all the would-be important citizens, stood in frozen rigidity; and bewilderment was in his eyes. He ignored the nervous twitchings of the club secretary's plump hand, and came and leaned against the railing. No one moved, but from the corners of their eyes they glared at him.

He stood looking out at the Sikh soldiers on the esplanade in front of us, sprucely drawn up on their slim legs, swathed in green and straight as young bamboos. They stood in the setting of a crowd as motley as the colours of their dress: brown Malays, black Tamils, Chinese whose lemon-yellow faces, beneath the equatorial sun, ripen perceptibly like an orange.

At that moment there was a rush for the bar. But I stood still, overcome with emotion, hesitating to approach one whom I cherished in my mind as I would cherish the memory of a dead friend. I had abandoned the idea of seeing him again because he had not answered my letters, and because the planters regarded him as an unapproachable misanthropist; at least I thought I had abandoned it. Now I realised that I had preferred not to see him again. Those fugitive war-time contacts that suddenly revealed the abysses of a man's soul, are an estranging influence afterwards, from fear of the mechanical intercourse of every-day. Him I still pictured in the light of the flares that seared the treacherous night around us. We were alone in a shell-hole; a chance encounter on the evening of a day of slaughter. Our machine-gun post was stationed near one of those calvaries that stand just outside every Picardy village. There the struggle is hottest; much blood flows at the foot of a crucifix. At that moment a vast silence had fallen, and the stranger realised that I was overwhelmed by that awful silence. He spoke to me and asked me questions. He knew what I was going through. He probed my flayed soul with gentle fingers that seem to pour out a corrosive drug. He seemed pleased to observe that I was as empty as that plain was ravaged. I had lost faith, love, and even self-respect; I had gone beyond contempt, which still offers some support, I knew no longer why I suffered since I was indifferent to life and to death. . . .

I fell silent again because I distrusted my voice, and it is ridiculous to talk heroics in a voice that trembles. I wondered if I were not like those old women who do not weep when they think of their misfortunes but only when they talk about them. The man's insight humiliated me and I felt ill at ease. But he, who understood, came to my rescue:

"At any rate you aren't one of those who say that it would not matter if one could be sure of getting out alive. A mean attitude. Listen, my young friend; it is delightful to be alive, and more delightful still to live on the edge of death. . . . Haven't you yet discovered that danger is only terrible at a distance? But here it is all around us, in the shadows, and it so enhances our sensations that the mere act of breathing is a joy. The moments of most perfect happiness are just those that are exquisitely precarious."

But this is a perversion of our talk; it did

not consist so much of words, as in the unuttered implications of our silences. It was like a direct contact between us,—a grasp of the encompassing world that lies beyond expression. But it is hard to recapture such matters afterwards; they are like a forgotten phrase of music. . . .

Later on, I remember, he spoke of far off lands that he had known, of a free and spacious life in the great equatorial forests. In that life, too, there had been anguished moments. He told me of some great beast, tracked for days, that suddenly turns and charges its pursuers; of a canoe spinning out of control round the bend of a river, when the jungle tips and turns as though the axis of the earth had shifted.

"But why," he said, "are you so excited by such stories? They are no finer than this immediate minute, and they hold no more of mystery. This is the hour of surprise attacks when the darkness begins to lift. Before I have finished this sentence, perhaps . . ."

"Stop!" I cried; "you'll bring them down on us! . . ."

"Did you ever find yourself," he went on calmly, "in open country, standing before a line of sputtering machine gun fire. The whole earth quakes; you are helpless in the meshes of that network of steel. Then you suddenly have the sense of disembodiment, an exhilarating impression. That is what is called heroism. It is no more than that."

"Do you mean to say you enjoy war?"

"No, I hate it. You've missed the point. You might as well say I was anxious to die."

He got up and went off. Went like a man insulted. It was just light enough to see one's way and he disappeared down a trench half blocked by a long bombardment. I could now see, at the edge of my shell-hole, the grass stirring under the acid morning wind, and further away a helmet moving off at the level of the ground, and I thought: "It's a tortoise . . . a tortoise. . . ." My head was going round, and my body was no more than a skin with nothing inside it. But someone brought me a drink that smelt of ether, and pierced like a cold keen blade.

That night of menace, and the dreadful days that followed, I can now recall without horror. Was it my encounter with the stranger helped me to the state of calm exaltation in which I endured them? Happiness in time of war consists in forgetting that you are a hapless, neglected little machine, and in ceasing to take any notice of the vermin that are devouring you body and soul. I had only been a short time at the front, and my enthusiasm of the first few days had been a mere mask of despair. Experienced troops are those who have acquired both prudence and indifference.

But they must also have recaptured the zest of life, for only those who love life are not afraid of death.

From that day forward I moved through the war like a sleepwalker on a roof. I set before my eyes a great vision, unreal yet very clear, that dazzled me. Malaya, evoked in the cold and darkness by one to whom it seemed like a dream, though he had indeed lived there for ten years, became for me a reality. I invented Malaya. I saw it in all its details, and I made myself so clear and detailed a picture that I did not feel its absurdity. My abode was a conical hut with a door like that of a dog kennel. Accompanied by truculent Malays, armed with spears and curious zig-zag swords, I roved through jungles bedecked with reptiles, and starred with humming birds.

Henceforth I knew that I should be given a chance of going to Malaya. It is useless to strain the will; a will too tense loses its elasticity. It is enough to be ready for the vaguest call of destiny, and then to build up the future in one's heart. Events will sort themselves out. Thus I lived in a sort of active fatalism; I clung to nothing, but my hands were open and ready to take hold.

The opportunity came. When war was over I went to Malaya; and I lived there for three years without ever falling in with the man who had lured me there. Now, at a stroke, he stood before me, like an incarnation of the dead who were that day commemorated.

He did not seem to recognise me and made as though to go away. I hurried up to him:

"Excuse me, Sir."

"Why, it's you, young man!" he cried; "Look here, don't call me Sir; it makes me feel so old."

He had put his two hands on my shoulders and the hand that I held out remained in the air.

"The fact is," said I, "I'm not even sure I know your name. . . . Rolain, is it?"

He seemed to acquiesce, but his only answer was a faint frown and a glint in his eyes.

"Did you get my letters? Letters signed Lescale?"

"Possibly," he answered; "I don't open many letters."

Once again I was at a loss. He added as if to excuse himself:

"You see, I don't live quite like everybody else. Today, for instance, I had to go to the bank to get the coolies' pay, and I arrive, like a fool, on a holiday. A curious ceremony. . . . But I'm glad to have seen an extraordinary thing: Europeans motionless and silent. What did it mean?"

"It's the anniversary of the armistice. It's in honour of the dead."

"They looked very uncomfortable. Were they thinking of the dead, do you suppose?"

"Yes," I said: "They were trying to look as if they were thinking about them. I speak from personal experience."

He grew thoughtful and said slowly:

"Anniversary. . . . Anniversary. . . . Do men so distrust their own memory?"

II

Rolain's plantation overlooked the Sanggor river at the point where it describes a great curve before emerging into the alluvial plain. The distance, from Kuala Paya, is only about a hundred miles. I offered to drive him back in my car.

He was not greatly impressed with my ancient motor. Though I bought it second-hand, it represents the savings of two years. Its organs hold together by wire and bits of string, but, once started, she moves subconsciously. We clattered victoriously up to the plantation in a cloud of steam.

An invisible plantation. At the end of a hibiscus avenue stood a little bungalow in a little garden on a little hill, all lost in an immensity of jungle that stretched away to the horizon like a stormswept sea, above which, towards the north, loomed the sombre mass of mountains.

"Where is your plantation?"

"On the other bank," said Rolain. "My idea was that a planter ought to have something to look at besides rubber when his day's work is over. A profession must not be allowed to become a penance. If I planted coconut trees, I should put rubber trees in my garden. It is a fine tree in isolation; and its flowers have a pleasant smell. . . ."

We were now on the veranda, and beyond a curtain of trees that edged the river, I could see the paler foliage of the *heveas*.

I understood why Rolain had come to choose that site, but the bungalow puzzled me. It was old and ramshackle. There was little furniture, and that was scattered about the place in such aimless disorder that it almost blocked up the veranda. A decayed crocodile skin, some melancholy stuffed animals, and a few snakes floating in turbid jars of alcohol, died a slow and second death. Mouldering sun-helmets, like mushrooms on a heap of tattered newspapers, lay strewn upon the tables. And over everything a layer of dust, and scraps of nipa leaves, which had fallen from the thatch.

On a placard attached very conspicuously to a partition wall I read the following declaration:

BEFORE GOD AND BEFORE MAN
ON MY FAITH AND MY HONOUR
I SOLEMNLY SWEAR
NEVER AGAIN TO TOUCH
ANY INTOXICATING LIQUOR
SO HELP ME GOD!

Bukit Sampah Estate
November 6th, 1922.

This was written in large capitals, a little unsteady in spite of the pencilled strokes that held them up. The word God was underlined in red ink, and the word Intoxicating underlined twice. The signature was undecipherable. Through the windows of the other rooms that opened on to the veranda, other such placards could be seen.

"I don't understand," I said, "where are we?"

"It's Stark who lives here," answered Rolain; "if you can call it 'living'. He is my manager, a half-caste."

"Forgive me, Rolain. I had been told you were mad, and when I saw this extraordinary house I believed for an instant it was true."

"Perhaps I am, if madness consists in acting differently to other people. But Stark is a reasonable man. He pursues—from a distance it is true,—a moral ideal. His placards bear this out. . . . Ah, here he is. . . ."

All that I saw at first was a vast two-storied sun-helmet, like an iron-plated dome. Then, as the man mounted the veranda steps, appeared a long sallow Eurasian face, a khaki shirt stained beneath the arms with two large discs of sweat, shorts, and red knees covered with curly tufts of hair. Stark was carrying a gun, a large bath towel, and with his other hand was dragging the long and flabby corpse of a monkey.

Rolain started. His expression, usually indolent and remote, became suddenly savage. I saw his eyes grow black and his nostrils whiten.

"Stark. . . . Have you taken to killing monkeys?"

"Hullo," said Stark; "I didn't know you were here. Yes, I'm collecting specimens again. But I've only killed one. What can I do with myself? A man must do something. Otherwise, ideas get into one's head, and one thinks and thinks . . . and then come cravings. . . . But I don't drink now, that's finished. Finished for good and all. Thank God."

His eyeballs quivered in a sort of mystic ecstasy, and he blew his nose in his towel.

"If you only knew how happy it makes a man to feel he has turned over a new leaf! I wrote to my dear old father yesterday, and I said: Your son has at last found the Way again, the righteous Way between the rocks of life. . . . Will you introduce me to this gentleman?"

And suddenly he burst into a sort of bellow: "Boooy!"

A prolonged cry on the same note answered him from the depths of the servants' quarters, and a Chinaman appeared, hurriedly donning a white jacket, and smoothing his straight bristling hair.

"What were you doing?" said Stark in Malay. "Here are two Tuans who have been waiting for an hour. Were you asleep, or smoking your filthy opium? . . . Those blasted Chinese wallow in vice—they have no sense of decency. Bring something to drink. I can only offer you ginger beer. I had a fresh case of whisky, but it's where it ought to be—at the bottom of the river. Now I'm at peace. Besides, I've taken the pledge. Alcohol is no temptation to me now. You know the saying: 'The word of a white man is worth its weight in gold'."

As he spoke, he kept on wiping his face and neck, and wrung the sweat from his soaking towel.

"We won't take anything," said Rolain, watching the boy approach with a tray of huge glasses. "I just wanted to tell you that I haven't got the pay money. . . . I'll send you a cheque next week."

"That's a pity," put in Stark.

"Why? Can't the coolies wait a bit?"

"Certainly they can. But they have to prepare for a festival and get their offerings for those old Devils of theirs. . . ."

"That's all right," said Rolain. "The festival of Ti-Vali isn't due for a fortnight. We are going on to my place—the car can stay here till Monday, can't it?"

Stark followed us, crestfallen.

"It's annoying, very annoying. . . . You can't go without having a drink. . . ."

As we were turning into the hibiscus avenue he twitched Rolain by the sleeve.

"I say, Monsieur Rolain, would you mind Joseph the book-keeper going to Kuala Paya with the cheque?"

"Joseph? Why Joseph?"

"Well—I don't much like going myself . . . because of the club—it's such a dangerous place for me. . . ."

"I understand," said Rolain. "Well, we'll try to fix that for you."

Rolain crossed the road and plunged into a half-hidden path that mounted the slope.

The jungle closed behind us.

We had not gone twenty steps before I stopped in astonishment.

Living as I did on the plains, I had known only those marshy forests where a man must walk thigh-deep in water, and pick his way through the network of roots: where the palm trunks bristle and the lianas cling: hostile silent forests that seem forbidden to all living things but mosquitoes and leeches. I knew nothing of the splendour of the mountain jungle with its red moss-strewn earth and steel blue ferns, its vast tree trunks, white and smooth or brown and rugged, shooting up for fifty yards without a branch. That jungle lives and breathes and murmurs, soaked in a happiness so deep that it wears the guise of indifference.

Ant-like I stood in all that vastness; it seemed to absorb me as though I had been a raindrop. I was in it and I felt its remoteness, I observed but I did not understand. Beyond the narrow circle of trees that barred my vision began the vast domain of mystery, and even around me in the play of shadow and the shafts of sun-light, among the shivering palm fronds and the rustle of the foliage that no wind can reach, in the dim agitation that encompassed me as subtle as the circulation of the blood beneath the skin, I discovered stranger mirages than those of the desert and felt the faint pressure of unknown forces.

Rolain too had stopped and stood silently behind me as though he feared to intrude. He knew that I would have liked to be alone. I wanted to thank him for having understood, and I laid a hand upon his arm.

The presence of another human being can be so irksome because it impels one to say what cannot be expressed. I thought this gesture would save me from speaking; but I felt that it was more significant than words. I still pretended to be looking at the jungle when I was but looking at the confusion in my soul. I did not know how to withdraw my hand. I must find some means to break the spell.

"I thought you lived on your plantation?" I said to Rolain.

"No," he answered, "I left it a little while ago. The war sickened me with orders and discipline. I could no longer give an order without thinking it futile or unfair. I half thought of selling the plantation, but it would fetch so little just now. Besides, I had a feeling that I should be selling the coolies as well."

The path turned and twisted up the slope and now and then took advantage of a great prostrate tree to span a ravine. As we advanced further into the jungle my first impression deepened. I saw no living being, and yet I felt I was at the very heart of an intense life: so startling an anomaly, that I could now better understand why the old legends peopled the forests with invisible beings, or plant-like entities veined with sap instead of blood. And as the light began to fail I guessed that those mysterious presences would beset us yet more closely with the darkness.

Soon, however, I became aware of a clearing just in front of us. The air moved more freely among the high branches and seemed to sweep them from the smooth surface of the sky, as a breeze dissolves a cloud. A snow-fall of light dappled the undergrowth. Rolain stepped aside to let me come up with him, and said rather solemnly:

"Here is my House of Palms."

We stood at the edge of an open space, and I saw a Malayan house, quite small and completely overshadowed by two great trees: a *kompas* with a stem so straight and tall that it looked slender, and an *ara* spreading bastioned roots to the edge of the jungle as though to check its encroachments. All the rest of the vegetation had been cleared except the palms, and the place looked like a vast hot-house glistening with delicate blades of silver. Tufts of *bertam* shot up on all sides like firework bouquets beneath the leafy downpour of the slim *nibongs*.

It was a house such as is still owned by the older fashioned rajahs: built of red varnished wood, with a pierced balustrade to its veranda, the design of which was repeated over the doors and partitions: long low windows with carved uprights, and an overhanging roof broadening at the edge in a curve like the side of a tent. Within, no furniture nor ornaments; but a profusion of mats and cushions and gold-embroidered hangings.

A young Malay, with bare chest and legs, and a silk sarong swathed about his hips, appeared in answer to Rolain's call. He still had the candid eyes and jolly round face of the small boys who gambol naked under the coconut trees in the kampongs.

"Get a bath ready, Smail, put out some evening clothes and curry us a chicken."

* * * * *

My first night in the jungle.

Smail had put out the lights. The night was dark. Lying near a window to get the cooler air I could not distinguish its square outline. The silence round the house had turned to a quiet murmur, like the sound of a moving river with far-off noises on its banks. I felt lulled and lost. It recalled my first night on the steamer that had brought me East. But the impression of launching into the unknown was now more marked. Then I passed gradually into a vague dream, in which I seemed to recover the pleasure that man must have felt in bygone ages when he crouched in some hidden lair.

And later on I heard the awakening of the jungle when the light of the rising moon began to filter through the foliage. It stirred with myriad rustlings that rose and fell like waves on sand. One feels that innumerable furtive creatures are everywhere in movement: a soundless tumult that sometimes grows more distinct. Thus, for a while, I heard a clear persistent signal, like a short sharp bark, and then an answering bark. It was a pair of panthers hunting, but that I did not know, and I tried vainly to decipher that strange music.

No better did I understand what then began to move in the long rectangle of the window, so full of baffling shadows. Once I could see quite clearly the trunk of a palm, but it vanished as I looked at it and reappeared at a distance. Strange shapes became visible between the trees—the swaying trunk of an elephant, a motionless head with staring eyes. I felt no alarm and yet I was aware of a sense of uneasiness that children feel when playing at hide-and-seek in dark corners. Remembering certain words of Rolain on the lure of mystery, I said to myself as I fell asleep: One might almost suppose that he has come to live here to enjoy the sensation of fear.

"So you heard all that, did you? And you didn't hear the tapir? He turned up last night. He was rooting and snuffling under the bungalow for a whole hour to see whether he could not find an odd bit of soap. . . . He has a sweet tooth, the tapir."

There were indeed large-hoof prints all round the kitchen.

"But if elephants come this way," I said, "couldn't they destroy your house?"

"They could," said Rolain, "but I hope they would not want to. I am less afraid of the intrusions of animals than of the most harmless human beings."

We were drinking our early tea on the veranda and throwing banana skins to the tri-coloured squirrels that played round the trunk of the great *kompas* tree. A troop of monkeys chattered in the branches. All around us were none but familiar animals and normal trees that did not move about. The head of a ravine abutted on to the front of the house, opening a deep cleft through which could be seen the fall of the hills down to a silver line that was the sea. The ridges were covered with a rich fur of jungle, patched here and there by small flecks of mange where men had scratched the surface.

"Civilization is climbing up," I said, "but from here its labours looks very futile."

"Men always believe," he answered, "that their civilization is the true and final one. Some do admit that a cataclysm may defeat it. But no one notices that all civilizations end by dying of boredom because the human ideal is ever changing. We are in the age of machinery.

It is very amusing but it will not interest humanity for long. We shall apply ourselves to subtler sciences. Children must grow up. . . . This jungle will witness other follies. . . ."

A discreet cough under the veranda.

"What is it, Karuppan?"

A tall Tamil, very dark and loose of limb, salaamed and offered Rolain a sealed letter which he held in both his hands.

"A letter from Joseph—my book-keeper, a fellow from Pondicherry. I wonder what he wants now; he's always whining about something."

He read the letter and handed it to me.

"I am going down to the plantation. Come along. But you might read that letter first."

DEAR AND HONOURED SIR,

After ripe and fruitful meditation I assume the garb of the humble suppliant in order to bring to your respectful notice that the new manager follows me daily with persecution, and my trouble is such as I am unable to describe. Neither person nor object is safe from his anger. He bursts into a rage over the merest trifles, until I begin to think I should be happier if I hanged myself.

My mind is torn asunder, and I am unable to fulfil my arduous duties, as I am also afflicted with an infirmity which decency forbids I should mention to you, Master, but which prevents me from assuming a sitting posture. I am thus plunged in the depths of misery.

Having regard to the frailty of my health, I have duly informed my wife, who weeps ceaselessly through day and night, that we shall proceed to embark on the 30th inst., and I have thus succeeded in comforting my spouse and children who walk in fear and trembling of the Demon of Iniquity.

Dear and most respected Sir, your Honour's estate is, however, the only one on which I care to stay, as it is the most perfect and the most beloved of all estates in the country. But you have abandoned your devoted servants. Many coolies shed bitter tears day and night.

Honoured Sir, I beg you will hold out the milk-white hand of Justice to save your sparrow from falling amongst thorns and thistles, and to come and see the new manager, for I dare not tell you how he has lapsed from Grace today, as you may see for yourself.

For which act of charity my family and myself will pray eternally for your Honour's prosperity.

Your obedient servant,

JOSEPH.

"Damn these half-caste swine," said Rolain, turning into the hibiscus avenue, "they always want to revenge themselves on somebody. But I am a little sceptical of Joseph's martyrdom. He was always in a misery of some sort. . . . Look—look to your left."

I turned just in time to see, at the windows of a little house below the path, an array of black heads and shining eyes: the tribe of Joseph on the look-out. They all vanished in an instant: under the house a few goats stood motionless and watched us.

"A nest of spies," said Rolain, "I expect that's what infuriates Stark."

As we approached the bungalow, a group of Tamils, who were waiting at the foot of the veranda steps, got up.

"What are you doing there?" asked Rolain in Tamil.

One of the men answered for the rest. He was apparently so important that he allowed himself to dress in the ludicrous semblance of a European. Completely so, except for trousers. His black jacket descended on to a shirt that fluttered over bare thighs. The others, being of a more humble rank, were draped in bright red and white stuffs. Not far away, crouched in attitudes of indifference, waited a small circle of very attentive women.

"Master, there has been a great riot on Master's plantation. . . ."

And the speaker plunged into voluble explanations. He talked and talked and seemed to draw no breath. Words rattled in his throat like pebbles down a torrent-bed.

". . . Then the wife of Sinnathamby said to the wife of Sinnasamy. . . ."

At these words the group of women began to cluck and chatter like a flock of guinea fowl.

"Tchi . . . Tchi . . . Tchi . . ." cried the men turning round indignantly, waving upturned hands.

"Where is the Manager?" asked Rolain.

"The master sleeps."

"Shall the judge sleep when justice is needed?" said Rolain to me. "If justice is needed he is generally to blame. Well, I'll go and collect him."

He walked up the staircase and I followed.

On the veranda, beside the corpse of his monkey, lay Stark, dead drunk. He was filthy with his own vomit, and from his soaked trousers, through the mattress on to the long chair, dripped a moisture that trickled in a thin stream across the floor.

I noticed that the placards had been turned to the wall. The snakes had sunk to the bottom of their jars: they floated no longer, for the jars were dry. . . .

There we stood, stiff and dumb. At last I turned away; my stomach was rising into my throat.

We sat down on the steps, and the Tamils whose eyes had been watching us at the level of the flooring, drew away.

Rolain wiped his forehead.

"I'll put the brute into a bullock cart," he said, "and send him off. He's got a brother somewhere in the district. But—I suppose I shall have to come and live here again. I hate the prospect, I confess. What a pity you aren't free. . . ."

"But I'll come," I cried. "I didn't like to tell you, but I might be out of a job any day. Rubber isn't doing well, as you know. They're cutting down expenses,—and of course they will very soon be able to do without me. Potter shields me as well as he can, but after all he is only a manager, and, as things are, he'll have to sack me one day."

"Very well," said Rolain. "Go right along to Potter and explain. He'll be delighted. Come back to-morrow. Now I must settle this affair."

He turned towards his men and spoke to them in Tamil. Stern at first, and their eyeballs slid from side to side; then ironical, and they hid their mouths behind their hands; paternal last of all, and they went away, cheerful.

III

Potter was a planter of the old school, one of those shell-backed pioneers of rubber who came from Australia or Scotland after a probation in Ceylon where they learned their job thoroughly by going through the mill on the tea plantations. He was feared by the coolies, but he knew them so well individually and in the mass, that he hardly ran any risk of being unfair. He had taught me the use of the rattan, which he regarded as the most expeditious and least humiliating means of correction. "For," he would say, "it is a mistake to locate the dignity of a man in the skin of his posterior. It is pure materialism. Prison is the only degrading punishment." So he continued the use of his rattan notwithstanding laws and regulations that increased every day in severity.

Not one of his coolies had ever lodged a complaint. Perhaps that was because he always managed to meet the victim on the following day. Then he would tap the man amicably on the head and shoulders and say:

"Look here, you silly fool, you forced me to beat you. You shouldn't do that. Do you think a father enjoys beating his children? But you are my child, and I beat you. Next time I shall flay the skin off you."

And the cooly, full of gratitude, would answer:

"You are my father and my mother."

Then Potter would turn to me with satisfaction: "A single cut with the rattan *and* a single kind word, that does them more good than any number of kind words. . . . Ay! and, I dare say, even more than any number of cuts with the rattan!"

But matters were not so comfortably settled when Potter had thrashed a bullock driver on the high road. He hated drivers because they were always on the wrong side of the road. Moreover the roads were never wide enough for his methods of driving a car. After bellowing at the man once or twice, he jammed on his brakes, jumped out of his car, seized the unhappy driver by his beard if he was a Bengali, by the slack of his trousers if he was a Chinese, and dumped him into the ditch while his bullocks trotted off. Usually no more was heard of the affair. But from time to time a Malay policeman was seen arriving at Potter's bungalow with a summons.

"Get out!" roared Potter from his veranda.

The Malay would crouch at the foot of the steps, roll a cigarette and cough every five minutes. At last Potter, exasperated by this insistent reminder, appeared at the top of the steps with fierce and glaring eyes.

"Let not the Tuan be angry," the Mālay would say.

"All right, old chap, but damn your eyes all the same."

And Potter signed the summons.

"Mr. Potter," observed the magistrate, Barnley by name, who was at the same time District officer, treasurer, tax-collector and so forth, "this is the third time today that your case has come up. You are always late."

"One can't get about on your roads," growled Potter, "they're full of bullock carts."

Potter pleaded guilty and gave no explanation, so that the affair might be more quickly settled. But the reading of the sentence provoked him to fury. He could not help growling: "Rubbish! To hell with your laws and justice!"

Two minutes afterwards he heard himself condemned to a hundred dollars fine for "Contempt of Court". Once more he blustered. At this point I used to try and distract his attention by pulling sharply at his sleeve; and Barnley, for his part, made haste to terminate the proceedings and disappear.

We would often meet Barnley once more as we entered a little village shop where drinks were sold.

"Whisky-and-soda?" he asked, as he saw us pass; "or beer?"

"I've had enough of your cross-examination," answered Potter; "you rotten little Jack in office. . . ."

Barnley wore his kindly placid smile.

"All right, Potter, now's your chance; you can say what you like, and relieve your mind."

"Pah! When you aren't perched on your bench and dignity, there's no fun in telling you how much I despise you."

And Potter would sit down gloomily.

"Mine's a whisky-and-soda," he sighed. "Long and strong."

* * * * *

I hurried back from Rolain's place to tell Potter the good news: I had been offered another job, and he could satisfy his Company's thirst for economy.

I found him just paying his coolies. This important ceremony was staged every month on the platform outside the rice-store. Seated at a small table Potter dominated a squatting crowd that cowered under his sombre looks. On that day he was infallibly in a bad temper. He had come back from town, where one meets old acquaintances and tends to linger at the Club bar. . . .

"They have drunk my health so often," he used to say, "that I feel quite ill; and so do they. And I hope to God they'll die of it."

I heard high voices on my arrival. A cooly had just asked for leave to go to Kuala Sanggor where his mother had lately died.

"Your mother's too fond of dying," shouted Potter. "It's a mania."

The cooly, who was a pert fellow, promptly gave notice and said he would leave the plantation at the end of the month.

Potter was down on him like a vulture and gave him a few cuts with the cane. Then he burst out abruptly:

"Damn me for a fool! Just when I have to reduce my labour-force!"

He called the cooly back.

"You can go at once. Go and bury your tenth mother. And then don't forget to go and see the Controller of Labour and tell him that I struck you because you gave notice in-ac-cor-dance-with-the-law."

But the cooly never went.

Another had deserved exemplary punishment.

"Your fault is serious," said Potter; "too serious for a thrashing. I shall cut you five dollars."

He took back a five-dollar bill.

"Do you think I'm going to keep it for myself? No, I have no right to keep it. But you have not the right to receive it. So . . . now observe the fearful consequences of your conduct. . . ."

And, striking a match, he set fire to the bill.

The man, who had not been much affected by the fine, when he saw this precious object vanishing into the void, this evaporation of so many good pints of toddy, this destruction of so many chickens that had not even lived, gasped and stretched out his hands in horror: and from the crowd arose the murmurous stir that follows upon great disasters.

"What? Are you giving notice too, Lescale? You ungrateful dog. I won't accept it. You'll have to pay a fine to the Company. . . ."

I might well have expected such a bark from the old watch dog. For Potter, who never received a letter from his Agency without grinding his teeth and described his Board as a pack of sharks, was the only man who really had at heart the interests of a business from which he drew a bare subsistence. His agents at Kuala Paya knew this very well and were not offended by the outbursts of this faithful rebel.

"Very well," I said, "I'll stay. But if I'm dismissed I'll bring an action against the Company. I suppose you know I'm due for a rise on the 1st of January?"

He glared at me as though I had been a slug.

"Don't talk nonsense. You know I've accepted a reduction myself. The conceit of these blasted little creepers! [1] Where's my stick?"

We had just reached his bungalow. He sat down wearily and rested his head on his hands.

"So you are going to Rolain's place. An odd fellow. The war upset his ideas. But he's

[1] Creepers: Young Planters.

a tough lad and a real planter—which is more than you'll ever be—and never afraid of anything. But I can't forgive him for having destroyed all my notions of the French character. Anyhow, beware of this type of man: either too cold or too hot, one never knows how to take them. . . ."

He called the boy.

"Bring the last bottle of champagne. There's nothing like champagne to put one right after an overdose of whisky. We'll drink to your success as plantation manager. Manager of Bukit Sampah Estate! Here's to you, old man! Blast those infernal agents for not letting me have an assistant! But you know I would have kept you on all the same, don't you? We could have managed all right on my pay. . . . Well, good-bye and God bless you."

IV

For my first few weeks at Bukit Sampah I was quite absorbed in my work as manager. I had first to learn the names of a hundred and fifty Tamil coolies, and of their headmen, the Kanganies; the character, capacity, and caste of every one of them, and then disentangle all the ramifications of their relationships.

Glad as I was to have a kingdom to govern, I made haste to display my little talents and apply my little theories. Every new manager of a plantation delights in demolishing his predecessor's pet institutions. It is essential to show that one can do better than he. His methods were bad. His favourites are disgraced. Indeed they often deserve it, just as they deserved their promotion. Thus, I made it clear to the Kangany of the jacket and shirt that he was not my Vizier, and that I did not care for his dress, or his air of superiority.

Stark had engaged a tall bearded Bengali who represented public authority and marched about the plantation like an Eastern King. I discovered that the principle task of this superb specimen was to see to it that the coolies disposed their excrements elsewhere than in the middle of the road. The Tamil does not like exposing his skin in sheltered places where demons and mosquitoes lurk. He prefers the open. All day long the Bengali concentrated his eyes and his mind in the search for exhibits, for each of which he received a reward of ten cents when he was able to denounce the perpetrator. So he was constantly on the look out for his exhibits, and also for the Estate Manager whom he delighted to honour with a grand military salute.

One morning, at break of dawn, I saw him squatting in the middle of the road, after which he disappeared. A cooly passed. The Bengali leapt upon him. Accusations, protests, and an uproar. . . .

The Eastern King was dismissed.

The plantation had not greatly suffered from my predecessor, and I found it in fair condition. All the clearing-up to be done was in the bungalow. Several bullock carts had indeed been filled with the refuse of the Stark Museum, for he carried this absurd collection about with him wherever he went; but I came in for a miscellaneous legacy of almost equal extent and value,—empty preserve boxes, bottle-ends, and old numbers of the *Christian Reformer*. The house and its immediate neighbourhood was strewn with such rubbish, and provided a lurking-place for cockroaches, whose antennae could be seen waving suspiciously before they dashed out and scuttled in frantic circles across the floor. The mattresses were moth-eaten and full of fleas, and for a week I scratched myself until I bled.

When the whole place had been thoroughly smeared with kerosene, I almost felt like setting fire to it. But the house was already altered beyond recognition, and I soon realized that it was neither unattractive nor uncomfortable.

Stark's boy had asked to be allowed to stay in my service, and I took him on because he was on the spot, and because I could see no difference between one Chinee and another. But though they are naturally careful, the Chinese are above all creatures of habit. When confronted with disorder and dirt, they adapt themselves to their surroundings with meticulous conscientiousness. I had to re-educate Ha Hek in the virtue of cleanliness, and he proved himself an apt pupil, intelligent, docile, and industrious. He had but one vice, and that a mild one, the vice of the virtuous; opium.

I then taught him to cook. He could fry sardines in lard, serve tinned salmon garnished with slices of raw onion, and make rissoles of anything, in such a way that I could never guess the ingredients. His sole idea of a vegetable was the large tinned pea of English origin, dyed a harsh green, as hard and dry as the droppings of a goat. They rattled on the plates like machine-gun bullets.

In the morning he prepared all the dishes for the day, and even for the day following: he merely had to warm them up when they were needed. Thus one could arrive at any hour of the day or night and shout "*Makan*"; and in five minutes a complete meal was ready on the table. This system had a good deal in its favour, for it often happened that I went out in the morning before it was light, and did not get back until three or four o'clock in the afternoon, famished.

Now, I insisted upon being given joints of meat, undeniable chicken cooked in its own skin, fresh vegetables, and fruits other than bananas. Ha Hek acquiesced. Every week he set forth in a bullock cart in search of these commodities. He constructed a little run for the fowls, and I made the estate coolies clear a good space of ground at the foot of the hill for a kitchen garden.

Thus was life organized on its material side.

* * * * *

The first periods of a new phase of life, like the earlier epochs in the history of civilizations, preserve, in the memory of them, the prestige of legend. The smell of wood and mould in the house meant little to me then, but I now know it to have been a precious perfume. It was like the smell of an old game of skittles, with which I believe I never played, but which was the most notable present that I ever had. The cleaning of the bungalow and better ventilation dispelled the smell, of which I only became aware when it had vanished.

My probation with Potter had accustomed me to Malaya. I had ceased to contemplate the country with wide eyes that see but do not understand; I thought I understood, and paid less heed to what I saw. Possession sobers a man until that day when he becomes aware that he is himself possessed.

At Bukit Sampah I discovered a new and more amenable Malaya. I lost the uneasiness of first initiation, and began to feel the calm joy that should accompany clear-eyed affection. From the top of my hill, I could discern, under its thick integument of jungle, the real structure of the land, its system of bones and muscles. Its personality was laid bare. Compared with this vast extent of undulating forest, the plain, with its plantations, villages, and fringe of mangrove-swamps, was no more than a parenthesis between the bend of the river and the slender arc of the sea. The swamps of the coast are not the true Malaya, but merely the sweepings of its mountains. I had to emerge from that litter to contemplate at last the huge virginal body sleeping in the sunshine.

The plantations that seemed so large, looked, as I now saw them, like little deserts in a limitless oasis. Rolain was right; a few years of neglect, and the jungle would confiscate the stock-in-trade of man, heveas from Brazil, oil palms from Africa; she would include the vanilla plants in her collection of orchids, and the bourgainvilleas and poinsettias would add to her adornments. . . .

The sounds of humanity came like brief intervals in nature's concert. From the plantation, which lay in a bend of the river, arose every morning the call of the muster horn that awakens the women to cook the rice. A little later a second call summoned the coolies to work. Sometimes, when their labours were over, they beat their tom-toms and sang until it was dark. A cart would pass slowly down the road. I heard the creak of the wheels, and a few phrases of a somnolent chant, broken by long silences, like the ramblings of a dream.

I slept with all my windows open. The first

blast of the horn awoke me, but I lay still on my bed awaiting the dawn, and listening.

It is the hour of deepest silence. The weary wild animals make their way to the springs to drink, and homewards to their lairs. The population of beasts that live in sunshine is not yet on the move.

There is a moment when nothing gives warning of the approach of morning; and suddenly a faint breeze, wafted from the sleeping earth, stirs the leaves with a sound like a rising curtain. Forthwith the "Te-te-goh", bird of the two twilights, scatters its three clear notes upon the air; one sharp note, and two conjoined, the last of which shoots downwards like a falling spark and vanishes. Tet! Te-goooh. . . . Morning and evening he can only snatch a few minutes hunting between the darkness that is void of insects, and the light that burns his eyes. But he is so happy that he celebrates his captures, and his voice seems to trace invisible arabesques in the sky. One by one, other birds join in, with tentative and timid calls and whistles. Then the trills grow more precise. Every instrument has its favourite refrain. Soon the rhythms blend into the cadences and chords of a whole orchestra of xylophones, fifes, and pipes, with now and then a little flourish on the rattle, or a beat or two upon the drum. . . .

But all this innocent unregulated babble from the birds is no more than a prelude. More sonorous voices are heard from far-off peaks. The sound is fluted, but full and flexible, like a flute with the calibre of an organ-pipe, and with all the 'cello's aptitude for sliding from treble into bass and back again. Voice blends with voice into a chorus. As it grows lighter, and the mists of morning fade, a long crescendo of questing cries rises from the trees, shriller and swifter and more passionate. And when at last the sun leaps above the mountains, it swells into a prolonged pæan of praise. This is the magnificent hymn of the gibbon monkeys.

So high an expression of feeling is soon exhausted. He who was the public's idol may shine more brightly, but his fame, once recognised, is as good as forgotten. A few revivals of fervour, a few isolated courtesies. Soon the sun looks down on silence. But then comes a discreeter murmur, the accent of a subtler delight; a sound that suggests the vibration of light itself. Fame has no longer need of praise, it lies in the heart of things; all day the jungle will quiver with the languorous trill of the cicadas.

From time to time one hears the chatter of the cocksure yellow-hammer who thinks any absurdity can be proved if it is only repeated ten times over, or the witty cadences of the black and white merle, who looks like a little magpie. The great hornbill passes, screaming as he goes, followed by its female—an affectionate ménage that expresses its affection in abuse.

But the most persistent bird is he who has nothing interesting to say. He is always far away and faint, but his interminable " takut-takut-takut . . . " is always in one's ears.

When the sky fades to the green of evening, just as at the close of a symphony the earlier themes are repeated, there is a brief recrudescence of cries from slumberous birds. And Te-te-goh heralds the returning darkness.

Then, in the rainy season, a confused chant like the bubbling of a cauldron, rises from the swollen river. The frogs, in an ecstasy, are offering up their evening prayer.

* * * * *

It rains a great deal in Malaya, but dark and dismal days are unknown. The sky exults, or sheds abundant tears.

About four o'clock in the evening a black stretched veil often rises from the horizon: so tightly stretched, that in passing over, it tears and breaks. Then the wind gets up, and in its wake roars the rain like another and mightier wind. Suddenly the blinds bang, the roof rattles, and the universe is effaced. The house, isolated in a sheet of moving water, is like a submarine heaving to the surface.

This lasts an hour or two, then the edge of the veil is lifted and reveals an angry sun. The steaming earth has grown a deeper red, the trees now tinged with gold, stand out in heavy masses against the intense purple of the flying clouds.

Malaya is content with this almost daily bath and for the rest of the time takes a sun cure. But in the rainy season she sometimes takes a tub on awakening. Unscrupulous young planters are delighted when this happens; morning rain means a day's holiday. For the rubber trees, like capricious cows, may only be milked in the morning. The milky latex will not flow in the heat of day; but if the trunks are wet, it flows too fast and runs to the ground.

When the weather was uncertain, a kangany came to the bungalow the first thing in the morning for my orders. I walked down with him to the muster ground where the roll-call was being held near the cooly-lines. The coolies were waiting in rows, the tappers on one side, the weeders on the other, and a little way off, a small self-conscious group of women whose condition kept them apart. A decision had to be made. I gazed at the sky with a professional air; I walked across to the tree and felt the bark. Sometimes, when the tapping had begun, a sudden shower fell. The distracted coolies rushed in all directions to collect in their buckets the latex that brimmed from the cups; and I tried to put a little order into the panic.

The gang of weeders needed a good deal of supervision, for at that season three weeds will grow while one is uprooted. It included the dregs of the population: old men, women, and children, who vied with each other in laziness and futility.

At the head of it was the oldest of the kanganies, a kindly and apathetic personage who enjoyed the indulgent respect of the entire tribe. He was a kind of universal grandfather. He alone had the right of an umbrella, which, from fear of spoiling it, he only used when the weather was fine. It was the insignia of his majesty. He lowered this canopy only in my presence, displaying a face like a parched medlar, a chest criss-crossed with white hair, and a flat brown belly, faintly lined, like an over-cooked griddle-cake. His name was Sinnamuttu, "little pearl".

The presence of the weeders was proclaimed from a distance by an incessant cackling, which Sinnamuttu, emerging from his dream, would break into from time to time with hoarse shouts of "Pésâthé! Pésâthé!" Silence! Silence! but they did not heed.

As soon as I appeared they all stopped talking, except Sinnamuttu, who, amid a dead silence, continued to call for silence.

The sanitary conditions of the place troubled me. The rains had brought a recrudescence of fever and bronchitis. But I had the happy idea of getting Joseph to help.

I had felt at first a certain antipathy for that flabby pock-marked frog-like countenance. The sight of it, especially in the morning, and the description of his morbid states made me feel sick. Moreover he had too rich a vocabulary. I was always expecting to be favoured with some unpleasing detail. So I cut our interviews short. But the spectacle of other people's troubles served as a relief in his case. He made a lugubrious but conscientious hospital attendant. A man looks after the sick all the better for being none too well himself.

We regard as excusable and even estimable in our own servants what would be intolerable in those of others. I discovered a certain kindliness in the expression of the man's face, and a certain savour in his speech. I was no longer annoyed at receiving sometimes in the morning a note that was always couched in the same terms, and was intended to convey that I should not see him that day.

Respected Sir,

I have the honour to bring to your notice that I have this morning taken medicine in order to restore my natural functions and to assure you of my entire devotion.

One day I was asking Joseph how his wife was, he answered: "She's poorly, Sir, very poorly."

"Why, what's the matter with her?"

"She's in the family way, Sir."

I tried to hide my amusement by chaffing him.

"What Joseph, at your age? . . ."

"Yes, Sir. . . ."

He wagged his head modestly.

"My flesh is weak. . . ."

V

> Tanam padi di-bukit Jeram
> tanam kedudok atas batu
> Macham mana hati ta-geram
> menengoh tetek menolak baju

Towards evening I often saw Karuppan, Rolain's Tamil gardener, passing near my bungalow. He was a gardener without a garden, whose only mission was to prevent the jungle from invading the compound. From time to time he brought in wood, or went to the village to buy provisions.

He was always followed by his wife who kept a respectful twenty paces behind him, as was proper. She was the handsomest woman on the plantation, slim but vigorous; and she walked like a queen.

I noticed that they made an aimless detour as they went back to their lines, which brought them in sight of my bungalow. When she caught sight of me the lovely Palaniai turned her head away, or half hid her face, but allowed a glimpse of a careless breast.

One day I made a sign to her. She hastened her step and disappeared behind the hibiscus hedge.

I could not see her, but between the branches, a little further off, there were small gaps which allowed a glimpse of the tender green of the grass. I waited for a moment, I could still see through them: she was watching me. I went round by the kitchen and came upon her.

A brief flight. I seized her by the wrists. She tried, but feebly, to shake off my grip. Her bracelets tinkled. Her averted face was buried in her shoulder, and she closed her eyes. I picked a hibiscus flower and put it in her dark and lustrous hair, which shone with the purple lights that are only seen reflected on women's hair in church.

I noticed that her closed eyes were turned in the direction of the kitchen. It was not her husband that she minded, but my boy. She let me lead her to my room. As she passed the mirror she put her hand to the hibiscus flower which was slipping from her hair. She sat on my bed as I went to shut the door.

"Don't be afraid," I said, but she shewed no signs of fear; and she helped my awkward fumbling hands to disengage her from the six yards of blue stuff that swathed her body.

Palaniai passed by nearly every day, her head piled with what she had just been buying in the village, hands of bananas, bowls or bottles, her arms swinging and her eyes downcast. She seemed to see nothing, and came in at the faintest sign.

I loved fondling her shapely arms, and that girdle of brown skin left bare between the hips and breasts by the dress of Hindu women. I was astonished by the contrast between the warm colour of the skin and its freshness to the touch. She let herself be stroked like a docile filly, and looked up at me with great deep empty eyes. Having no modesty, she was in no sense immodest. Her simplicity brought me much deep and innocent joy. A woman is no more than a delicacy, sweet or sour, and more or less well got up. The choice sweetmeat that Malaya offered me, on behalf of India, resembled one of those chocolates wrapped in variegated paper and filled with a sugary liqueur.

The visits of Palaniai were brief. She always had good reasons for going away again as soon as possible. However she sometimes agreed, if I insisted, to stay until the following day. But as soon as I was asleep she disappeared, and I found her lying on the floor beside my bed, as though she considered it improper to sleep at my side. She left behind her a warm musky odour, faintly cloyed by coconut oil, which brought me odd dreams.

In the morning I helped her to dress in the long piece of stuff which was her only garment. Half of it, to begin with, had to be gathered between the fingers into a sort of closed fan, which was then laid against her right hip. The rest was carried twice round the waist, very tight, and then diagonally across the chest over the left shoulder. The gold edging dropped in front slantwise to the ankles.

Dressed and with her hair in order, she

seemed to think it polite to stay for a little while. She liked to finger my toilet table but inspected what stood on it with a caution inspired by respect and perhaps intensified by the bottle of ammonia. Then she would ask my permission to go.

It was noteworthy that she never asked for anything else, and when I happened to finger her jewels, made no allusion to those she lacked. Her arms and ankles were loaded with bangles, but they were ill-matched and of unequal value. On one side of her face a heavy circlet with silver pendants dangled above her shoulder; on the other was nothing but a little plug in the lobe of the ear. This inequality was indeed made good on the side of the unadorned ear by a tiny golden flower pricked into the wing of a nostril. But I would have liked to see, like a trembling dewdrop at the end of that straight little nose, one of those light gems that set off the delicately moulded lips and flashing teeth.

I happened just at that time to come across a moonstone I had bought in Colombo for a girl friend left behind in France. But this girl was very far away. My wish to send her the jewel had dwindled into an intention to bring it her one day, and it was now lying among some trouser buttons in a drawer. Palaniai was delighted with it. She poised it on her hand, whose darkness intensified the dancing blue radiance in the stone, and then, when she raised it to the light, was astonished to see, the radiance fade as though this drop of sky had vanished into the blue.

I should have liked to test Palaniai's disinterestedness a little longer. But this first gift prevented my ever knowing whether she came because she really liked me, so that I was merely left with reasons for making other presents. My taste for symmetry brought her another ear-ring. Then, as I had noticed among sundry small objects that she carefully rolled up in the folds of her garment, something that looked like a bit of looking-glass, I gave her a mirror in which she could see her whole face. For, apart from her reflection in the wells, she had never seen it but in slices.

Generosity breeds jealousy. The more eagerly presents are accepted the more one regrets having given them. They eclipse the giver. Palaniai became mercenary; I despised her a little, and grew more set upon her. I made a few allusions to Stark. She did not understand at first, and then protested with an indignation that seemed genuine. But when I mentioned Rolain's name, she clasped her hands in a gesture of adoration.

It so happened that Ha Hek unwittingly surprised us when we were together. Palaniai, who was naked, drew back against the partition, but the planks were white-washed, and she shewed up as conspicuously as a fly in a bowl of milk. Ha Hek, however, passed her as though she had been invisible. He had an impersonal air which made me regard him as less a living being than an automaton. But I observed his disapproval one day when I saw him sniffing rather dourly at my pillow.

VI

One of the strictest articles in Potter's moral code was that a planter must not "touch" his female employees. "Not that there is much risk of upsetting the coolies, but it might make you unfair." In any case Potter seemed to think that this rule was to be absolutely observed by any man of less experience than himself. I deduced that, for the time being, one's attentions should be confined to the women of the neighbouring plantations.

I had an uneasy feeling that my adventure with Palaniai, so soon after my arrival, might annoy Rolain. There was a sixteen eyed Argus in the house of Joseph to tell him all about it. Ought not I to tell him myself? I decided that I would. Then, as he never came, my resolve faded. I was not without excuse; solitude, no neighbouring plantations. . . . And Palaniai, though but little of a gossip, would come occasionally with a scrap of news. I soon persuaded myself that I only received her at night for a useful and commendable purpose, like a good planter who spares no pains to know what is going on in his domain.

Native women who are secretly admitted into the Master's house usually dissemble the fact with enough ostentation to make all the rest aware of their glory. They soon learn to take advantage of the treacherous reflection of mirrors: and a cry of alarm escapes them, when needed, at the proper moment. Palaniai, on the contrary, was discreet. I thought at first that she did not care to stress the obvious. I believed our intrigue known to all the coolies; in any case Karuppan must be aware of it. But as she continued to take a thousand subtle precautions to avoid discovery, I began to devise a thousand subtle reasons to explain them. Then I told myself that she was a mystery maniac—one of those people who go through life with only two obvious occupations, of which one is to hide the other.

The truth was simple, but I could not have discovered it. It was revealed to me later by a remark of Rolain's: "Karuppan and Palaniai are in love with each other, you know . . ."

That made me smile at first. He looked at me and understood.

"You?" he said, "For them you do not count. You are beyond caste. Palaniai brings you merely a propitiatory offering, and Karuppan troubles himself no more than men of ancient days who gladly gave their wives to a god with a taste for mortal women."

"But why hide herself, then?"

"Just because she does not love you and does not want to be misunderstood. Love likes to display itself: dissimulation shows that love is labouring under some unnatural inhibition."

I realised from many indications that came back into my mind that Rolain was right. But I was more vexed than flattered to play the part of a deity so little esteemed.

"What does seem to me unnatural," I said; "is for a man to give the wife he loves to someone that she does not love, for purposes of profit."

"I don't think," said Rolain, "that there is quite so much calculation in the matter. He knows that his wife is entirely his. Do you think those husbands more reasonable who abandon their wives' minds to every sort of influence, and are only roused if they lose the bodies too?"

"But, after all, the body is not without importance. Have you thought of the child that may be born?"

Rolain reflected for a moment.

"Yes, that is the only argument. The child. . . . Jealousy is always the instinct of reproduction. All those agonised lovers who believe they don't want any children are really tormented by the myriad children hidden in their marrow. Their fever is the work of germs, like malaria. But if Palaniai has a child it won't be yours."

"How do you know?"

"It won't be yours as long as she doesn't want it to be yours. But I don't know her secrets."

He added after a silence:

"I still know very few of the secrets of Orientals."

* * * * *

Cultured Orientals esteem us much in the same way as we look at the Anglo-Saxons of America: they see precocious children, despotic, crude, and naively self-sufficient, who shew a great deal of imagination in their often dubious sports.

We preserve our prestige with fallen nations. The ancient Tamil peoples, worn out by centuries of misery and forced by famine to emigrate to Malaya, recover in their association with us ideas that they had forgotten,—just as old men in second childhood like to get the younger generations to read aloud to them the books of their boyhood. We bring them our latest knowledge, our discoveries, and our fairy tales. We tyrannise over them with unconscious egoism: and they reply to our condescension by a blind admiration.

Sometimes, indeed, we are loathed; for old men who do not adore children, hate them.

I instinctively understood the Tamil character: it is like our own. Careless, loquacious, excitable, and docile,—they recalled my comrades in the war.

Every day I observed how easy it is to secure good-humoured obedience by the aid of a trifling mark of rank, or even a differently coloured skin. Love your fellow-men a little, and they will adore you.

Stark's system of government was based on mistrust. He looked for laziness, insubordination, drunkenness, and strife; he pretended to suppress them, and only succeeded in creating the further vices of cunning, deceit, and ill-will. Too many laws and regulations stifle the sense of good and evil. No one looks beyond his own personal interest; and nothing matters except the evasion of punishment: The plantation was an overgoverned state, as are all the European States of today; and the men were an army demoralised by discipline.

When I went to talk things over with Rolain and ask his advice, he quoted the precept of old Lao-Tse: "Govern a great empire as you would cook a small fish."

I was not governing a great empire. My task was easy. Gradually I saw the return of confidence and emulation. Without abandoning the cane, I used it rarely, and never when I was conscious of being angry. The coolies believed in my justice. I could say to one of them: "You will come to the bungalow tomorrow with a rattan, and I will thrash you." He came, and I thrashed him.

I performed a few miracles, which increased my prestige. They are good asset towards a new code of morals. With my bare hands I picked up pythons (when of convenient size), a snake much dreaded by the coolies. I cured by Calmette serum a man who had been bitten by a cobra, and for whom his wife, who was constantly complaining of him, had begun to intone the chant of death; that shrill and sobbing litany of praise which every Tamil woman can improvise, and which does less honour to the virtues of the husbands than to the wives' imagination and their self-command in grief. Finally I sobered a drunken man instantaneously, with a small glass of ammonia. This was the miracle that caused the most sensation.

Rolain came to the Ti-Vali festival. The temple was decorated with flowers and festoons of coconut fronds, from which swung little plaited birds. We were garlanded with jasmine and marigold, and sprayed with attar of roses. Coconuts were broken in front of the glittering idols and the modest stone that represents the god of the pariahs. The scared goats were purified by the sprinkling of coconut milk and then sacrificed. One man held the horns, another the hind legs, and the neck was severed with a single stroke. The bodies quivered in a gush of blood, and the heads bleated voicelessly upon the ground.

And on the second day, when I was at Rolain's house, we saw a vast procession climbing upwards through the half-light of the jungle, and suddenly from the forest-edge burst forth a machine-gun volley of tom-toms and the strident arrows of trumpet calls. A joyous crowd scattered beneath the palms. The compound, in its array of fresh colours looked like a blossoming garden. The handsome Mukkan, clad only in a scarlet loin cloth, balanced upon his head a large tray of presents: goat-flesh, bananas, shaddocks, little green limes that bring good-luck, and bottles of beer and gin, without which latter it would seem that happiness, for Europeans, is incomplete. Once again we were soused with perfumes.

The concert began. The drummers scraped the tom-toms, the trumpeter, with dilated face and cheeks, squinted over his instrument. Bayaderes danced, as lovely as Palaniai, but with a lither and more lively grace, and I hardly recognised in them the youths whom I saw every day at work. A human tiger, saffron striped, bounded about the compound where only royal tigers rove. The house was beset by an array of radiant laughing faces in whose friendly eyes a dark light flashed.

II

THE HOUSE OF PALMS

II

THE HOUSE OF PALMS

I

Padang perahu di-lautan
padang hati di-pikiran

UNFORESEEN events, fresh faces, the discovery of a more magnificent Malaya, had entertained me all through the long rainy season, just as a picture-book can outlast a childhood. Time stood still, and Potter and his plantation were buried in the past.

But, insensibly, routine has come upon you; and you drop into the daily round. Once more a smooth monotony of days in which each one slides into the next. It is only to nomads that life seems long.

And yet, as I remember it, my time at Bukit Sampah does not seem like an epoch in my life. I have the impression that, at the edge of the ageless jungle, I inhabited eternity. In Malaya the seasons are hardly distinct. You do not die a little every year, as in Europe at the end of Autumn. You cease to think of date or time. You lose the habit of cutting up your life into sections and stitching them together again to the ticking of a watch. Only the contrast of day and night suggests that the earth has not ceased to revolve. But those days, those nights, always equal, all alike, seem to partake more of space than of time. There they still are, motionless as I survey them, and it costs me an effort to locate my recollections on that chess-board.

Sometimes I dropped in on Rolain, whose solitude I had at first intended to respect. He baffled me by his casual greetings, his long silences, and his abrupt remarks. All this seemed to me contradictory. Because he was quite different from all men I had known, I thought him very complicated. I wondered why I liked him. Our affection does not take account of our friend's personalities; it tries to remodel them by its own ideal, or demands at least that they shall make some semblance of conforming to it. Accustomed to hypocrisy by our education, we do not try to understand the spoken words, but to catch the purpose behind them. Thus, words have only an indeterminate meaning, which we may adjust as it suits us all along the scale of analogies and contraries. This masquerade of language is what creates the solitude of man.

Rolain was a mystery to me for two reasons; his simplicity, and my affection. For the very warmth of our hearts, like our breath on a window pane, lays a mist over transparency.

I remember arriving one evening at Rolain's house in a high state of excitement. I had many things to tell him; but as his habit was, after a faint nod, he seemed to have forgotten that I was there. I turned in a circle, like a beast in a cage. He was reading.

"What are you reading?"

"The Bustanu s-Salatin."

"You're only interested in the Malays," I said, "A fine sort of people—lazy, deceitful, and vain. That's my opinion."

"You say 'my opinion' as that carpet would say 'my place'," said Rolain calmly, and went on reading.

My irritation against the Malays was of recent date. Hitherto my feeling for them had been one of indifference. What interests us is what serves our interests—and the Malays are not servile. Obliging, certainly: but that is little. We are too practical to be content with that. We refer to the population of a country as "labour", just as we should like to describe the entire animal kingdom as "cattle". But the Malays do not at all wish to be considered in this light. Their point of view is contrary to ours. They can easily get their daily rice by working one day a week and they ask for no more. All fatigue is useless and harmful. Life is long,—why hurry? In the morning, perhaps, they visit their nets along the river or their traps at the edge of the jungle, and there they may find some beast of the waters or of the forest, which the Tuan Allah has allowed to be caught, so that their bodies may become man, and their souls, in the souls of men, may learn to know Him better. If He has not so willed, it is because He has caused a hand of bananas to ripen in the corner of the kampong, or there will be some young shoots of bamboo, an excellent vegetable, waiting to be cut. They are sure to find something that will serve to season their rice. Tomorrow, perhaps, fate will be kinder, and there will be more to eat. . . .

I did not know what to make of this people. Their carelessness seemed to me a matter for both admiration and contempt. But I always regretted the Malays of my imagination, as depicted in our stories of adventure. The wild pirates that infest the narrows of the Sunda islands. . . . And I had found only these little placid and polite men. They had destroyed my illusions, like those great pythons shown to children in menageries, inert at the bottom of their tanks.

At Bukit Sampah the Malays lived on the river banks. From the windows of my bungalow I could see the grey roofs of their huts under the tall coconut trees. Often, indeed, I peered through my fieldglasses at certain young women who came every day to take their bath on a raft moored to the bank. Naked under a short flowered sarong knotted across their breasts, they bent down to draw water, and then stood with up-raised arms while the water gushed over their rounded shoulders. The transparent patterned stuff stuck to their skins like tattoo marks. Towards evening when school was over, the children from the kampongs in their turn appeared on the raft, gambolled, dived, and swam, and the river was full of little golden frogs.

This population lived on the edge of the estate. Malays and Tamils met only on the road, did not speak, and seemed hardly to see each other. Frontier incidents were rare and I did not have to interfere. I thought the peace would never be broken, and then suddenly my nights had been disturbed by continual alarms. Awakening from a sleep haunted by images of war, I heard strange noises; men gliding through the brushwood, creaks and murmurs, and suddenly the sound of a heavy missile crashing through the branches. Then—shouts and cries, and a wild stampede through the undergrowth. I hurried out on to the veranda. Leaning with my elbows on the railing I could see, between the trees, shadows wandering across the kampongs and crouching on the river banks. I stayed where I was, wondering at the cause of this furtive agitation, and swarms of mosquitoes came and fastened on my legs.

I had sent for Joseph.

"What's all this?"

"Ah, Sir, it is because the Malays' durians are ripe. Can't you hear them falling all over the place around their houses?"

The durians were ripe. That event explained everything, for the smell of that fruit seems to madden men as valerian maddens cats. The lure of papaws, custard-apples, mangoes and mangosteens, can be resisted, but where durians were concerned it was, as Joseph observed, *very impossible* to keep the coolies in hand. They spent their nights on the look out, slept at their work, and suffered from colic. I purged, threatened and punished. But every morning the ground near the lines were strewn with spiky rinds, debris of the nightly orgies.

I had come to talk to Rolain about these incidents. The matter was becoming serious. Some Malays had pursued one of my Tamils as far as the plantation, and had hammered him on the head with the fruit of his larceny, which was spiked like a mediaeval mace. I had then taken my coolies' part, for as soon as fighting begins justice yields to patriotism. The Malays had behaved badly; they had replied to my threats with offensive courtesy, humouring me as if I had been a peevish child, and Rolain had dismissed me with a shrug of his shoulders. I pondered bitterly.

Rolain was losing interest in his plantation. When I talked to him about it, he did not even listen. I would act without consulting him. My duty was to protect my coolies. Potter would never have tolerated such invasions of his territory. These Malays set on poor

Virasamy and refused to answer my questions. They were a pack of ruffians and cowards. . . .

"I forgot to add," I said to Rolain, "that the Malays are cowards as well."

"Ah?" he answered with a smile.

Then:

"Have you ever tried to strike a Malay?"

No, I had not tried. And I was well aware that I did not want to go so far. Even Potter. . . . When Potter, jumping out of his car, found himself confronted by a Malay driver, his anger at once dropped a few degrees, and the terrible cane became an innocent switch. The reprisals were confined to a bombardment of abuse, for which divers languages supplied the ammunition: "*Ni bloody bodoh. . . .*" The Malay, as though shocked by such a display of ill manners, surveyed Potter with an absent air, and urged on his oxen by negligently twisting their tails between his toes. Potter vented his suppressed activity on the accelerator, and his hairy wrists, as they gripped the steering wheel, seemed to shake the whole car on which he wreaked his vengeance by furious driving.

"Insolent brute! I ought to have killed him. . . ."

Rolain, however, his eyebrows ironically raised, had followed my thoughts.

"Did your friend Potter . . ."

"Look here," I broke in; "I'm sick of you. You are always right and you know everything that's in my mind. You sit there and squint at me as if I were a doubtful egg. It's impossible to talk to you. You don't even allow me to have an opinion."

"Listen, old man," said Rolain quietly; "a fit of hysteria is not an opinion. You must not argue like a journalist. Do you remember? The Germans stank because they were at war with us. Their lice were more loathsome than ours. And here are you saying that the Malays . . . Do you know them . . . ?"

"Oh, you are right," I cried; "perfectly right. I won't have any more opinions. You shall tell me what to think, and I'll be your disciple."

Rolain was never taken aback by the sudden tackings of my mind.

"One can only guide a disciple as far as himself. And sometimes that is a very long way. . . ."

He reflected a moment.

"One never does, really, reach oneself. That is indeed an argument for the immortality of the soul. . . . Have you noticed that men have settled ideas only on subjects they have never thought about?"

* * * * *

I proved a zealous but restive disciple—a kangaroo who loves none but his trainer and is always ready to box with him.

Rolain talked little, and only did so to express

—or merely to suggest—ideas. I was not used to that kind of conversation. A conversation is as often as not simply a game in which several players join, to take stock of facts. An innocent and peaceful game which one could just as well play by oneself. With Rolain I was constantly baffled; I felt as though, having served him a ball in a tennis match, he had returned me a bird on the wing.

Thus it was, indeed, that I figured Rolain's thought; as a living thing, not unlike the explosion of a shell and not amenable to physical laws, remote, intangible. I saw it darting towards me—it was black. A stroke of the wing, and it was white. If it happened to alight sedately by some frequented path-way of the mind, I cried—At last! I can photograph it now! But while I was on its track, it had dived again into a whirl of fantasy, in which, one must admit, some purpose was discernible.

"Stop," I would say, "you go too fast, you skip too many difficulties. I can't reach the ultimate consequences of an idea before I have even understood it."

"But," said Rolain, "explanations simply make a thing more intricate."

"Yet language was made for explanation."

"Language has drowned thought by clinging to it. The richest languages are the least subtle. They aim at attaining the essence of an idea by multiplying fine distinctions. Vain complexity. . . . Our spiritualists try to make the spirits speak and are answered by absurdities, for a spirit cannot feel at ease in our vocabulary. We should do no more than interpret the thoughts that hover in the air about us. That is what the Malays do. Malayan spirits are dumb: but the Malays understand them."

"And yet," I said, "I understand you better when you are kind enough to explain."

"I can convey to you," said Rolain, "the rudiment of an idea, but if I want to go more deeply into it, I avoid expression. Oncc let an idea be moulded and it hardens like a snow-ball; you can only break it, or wait until it melts."

* * * * *

"Rolain, I should like to ask you . . ."

A sort of shyness made me stop.

Rolain surveyed me for a moment.

"Why hesitate?" he said. "You launch into the void, and then you wind up your thread again like a spider. It is very rude to hesitate when you are speaking to a friend."

"Well, I sometimes feel a doubt . . ."

"Doubts are always justified."

"No, but I'm sure . . ."

"Sure of what? . . ."

"I am quite sure," I went on dubiously, "that the day you came to the club at Kuala Paya you did not recognise me."

"Of course I did," said Rolain.

The reckless spider revolves in the wind at the end of its thread. He had recognised me. He knew me but he would not know me. If I had not hailed him, Rolain would have gone without troubling to walk across the room to me. What sort of man is this who calls himself my friend? He merely endures me, or makes use of me.

"Well, that's the end of it," I thought. "There is nothing more to say: I'll write to him tomorrow, I'll go back and work for the benefit of unknown people whom one can neither hate nor love. . . ."

"I remembered very well," Rolain went on, "the wretched and disgusted little soldier who said he did not mind whether he lived or died; but prayed that he might die, and wanted —didn't he?—to live. I kept him deep in my heart, with several others. I did not wonder where he was, since he was there. And when I saw you alive, and outside myself I felt a thrill, but not more so than if I had been told that instant that you were dead."

"How awful," I said. "A man who can say such things loves no one but himself."

He answered, with a shrug of lassitude:

"Don't you understand that if I live alone it is because I am too fond of those I love. You should not force such confidences."

And he went on in a strange undertone:

"There are creations so pure and so aloof, that in their presence we are, as one may say, outside ourselves. That is holy ground. What we learn by heart we tear out of our very hearts. . . ."

"Ah, you are always thinking of yourself," I answered. "You know me by heart and you are disappointed. And no wonder. But if it's a matter of indifference to you, for my own part I prefer not to be dead."

I would not leave him time to answer.

"Listen. When I went off to the war I merely thought of killing Germans. But, later on, when I heard the rattle of our machine guns I thought that a Goethe or Schumann might be in the trenches opposite."

"What a rotten soldier you must have been to think of such things. . . ."

"Not at all. I was. . . "

"Just so. Only bad soldiers and good soldiers are of any interest. The rest could have been killed without much loss. But then the earth would be a desert."

"Let us go back to the point," I said. "Is it a matter of indifference that Goethe and Schumann should die before their genius asserts itself?"

"Perhaps not to us," Rolain admitted. "But it is no more than a postponement. Time that seems lost counts for nothing in eternity."

I reflected a moment. "Rolain, I think I understand. I have had the same feeling, a sort of apprehension when I thought that

I might meet you again. . . . But I would not have dared to tell you so."

* * * * *

Sometimes, when work was over, I happened to go straight up to Rolain's house without stopping at my bungalow.

"Here comes the overworked planter, all dripping with professional sweat," Rolain would say. "You'd better go and wash it off."

Rolain's bathroom was a flat stone on to which a spring gushed through a bamboo pipe. I had only to walk down a few steps and stand under the falling water. Soaked in that water and in filtered sunlight I stood in a rainbow. I lingered, naked, beneath the palms. Then I emerged with muscles eased and blood purified as if my veins had absorbed that swift and luminous chill water.

Smail brought me a sarong and then went up to prepare the drinks. Some porous jars stood in the shade of the veranda in which the water retained, with its freshness, an earthy savour. Smail knew how to temper its sharpness by an admixture of the luscious juice of granadillas: and we added to this serum a little gin or kirsch.

"A drop of spirit in matter," said I.

The drop of spirit. . . . I might say I found it in those long evening talks. Enlivening intellectual gymnastics that cured my weariness much better than massage. I gave my body a holiday. I forgot it. I recovered it afterwards, emerging soothed and as it were transfigured from the chrysalis of slumber.

We talked and talked. Sometimes, on my way back to my bungalow after one of these discussions, I suddenly bethought myself of new arguments. At every turn of the path they sprang up in my mind, straight and solid like the tree trunks all about me.

There (I thought) he couldn't find an answer to that. . . .

The jungle was darkening: I had just time to get out of it before black night fell.

I walked a little further down the steep stair-like path. Below, between the branches, I could see the lights on my veranda. Ha Hek lights the lamps. Dinner. Alone. . . . And then, when it was really too late, I ran back to Rolain's house, stumbling over roots and ant heaps, tripping over thorned lianas, half-seeing, panting, with packs of tigers at my heels.

"The Tuan is brave," Smail would say, as he saw me arrive.

Sometimes, when I had stayed too late and had not even attempted to go home, I would resume hostilities in the middle of the night, if I heard Rolain move on the other side of the thin partition.

"Are you asleep?"

"No."

"Listen: I wanted to say——"

"Look here, my lad, you have to get up at five o'clock; you ought to go to sleep," objected

Rolain. But he came, bringing cigarettes, and sat on a corner of my mat.

I never could quite get the conversation back to the point where we had left it. Rolain thought it was never worth while trying to exhaust a question, since we would ourselves be exhausted long before.

I had sought in him a doctrine which I would gladly have contested and finally adopted. But I realised that it was I that made him seem didactic, just as, in summing up our conversations, I have given them a sententious turn so that I hardly recognise them. When we came back to the subject his point of view had usually changed.

"But you said——"

"In conversation," he would answer, "one must always say a thing is or is not so. But human affirmation is merely a hypothesis. Every belief should be provisional. . . ."

Thus, I had chosen a guide who led me haphazard into a search that ended nowhere and who often lost me on the way. When at last I found out that he was trying neither to convince me nor to impose on me I became more acquiescent; and less sensitive because he always spoke with sincerity. If I had made some error of judgment in dealing with the labourers, and had admitted to myself that it was a silly mistake, I told Rolain about it; he said "That was silly of you;" and I was not offended. Thus, little by little, our friendship was established, for the mark of friendship is in the telling of truth, and its acceptance.

II

Murai gila jadi tekukur
ajaib hairan hati tefekur

"The Tuan is not in," said Smail.

"Where is he?"

"Gone. He often goes off into the forest, quite alone. . . ."

I lay down on a mat. After a bath, a siesta is pleasant in this shady retreat. The jungle also rests at this time of day; I can hear its gentle breathing.

Smail comes back.

"Would the Tuan wish to drink?"

"No, later on."

What have I been dreaming about? The dreams of afternoon are so vague and swift. . . . Some young people were kissing in the shade, and I had hidden myself to watch them. Why has Smail awakened me?

Chuk! Chuk! Chuk! . . . That was the noise of kissing I heard; the homely little lizards chasing each other across the walls. I like to observe the lively tricky little creatures. The males are smaller, but move faster because they do not wriggle so much. When a female is caught and bitten on the neck, there is no more sound of kissing. They stiffen into a tortuous embrace. Other males gather round to watch them, and then go hunting in their turn. There are some, too, who only chase flies. They advance straight upon their victim but stop to hypnotise it before the final leap.

Smail kept coming in and out. He closed the wire shutters to prevent the mosquitoes coming in with the evening breeze; he lingered to put a book in its place; he asked me the time. A strange question for a Malay! He had certainly something to say. But I guessed that he would say nothing if we did not first talk of something else.

"Smail, do you know why the *chichak* stops before he jumps on the fly?"

"To leave him time to say his prayers to Allah," he answered without hesitation.

"Do the animals pray to Allah?"

He seemed shocked at my ignorance.

"How should they not?"

"And the rice that you are going to cook, does that pray too?"

"The Tuan is laughing at me."

"No, Smail, I want to know what the Malays think. Doesn't the Tuan Rolain ask you questions too?"

"White men," said Smail, "ask the sort of questions that little children ask." And he added: "We eat the rice, but we do not eat the rice's soul."

This, to me, meant nothing. I ought to ask if the soul of the fly is eaten. But the word that

I render "soul" is a very awkward word. An animal soul, a vegetable and even a mineral soul—how are these notions to be understood? Though my logic is at a loss, I dare not assume that Smail is a fool. What he says may contain a truth, and must in any case possess a meaning. My instinctive logic tells me so. Thus when I was a child I reverenced the absurd. At church, during the litany, I repeated with everybody "*petit piano, petit piano*", until the day when my mother revealed to me that I ought to say "*priez pour nous*".

Was the answer really incoherent? I was not sure. How should I find out? I did not talk Malay well enough to press the point. In this country I was a child of three years old.

Malay is the easiest language. Everyone says so. It is also one of the most difficult. Rolain says so. When he talks to Smail, I lose myself after the first few words. Many of them I recognise, but they are so oddly arranged, and seem to emerge by chance like the numbers in a lottery. . . .

Smail knew how to adapt his language to my ignorance. He used the pidgin Malay of the white man, and what he was able to tell me made me wish that he could tell me more.

For the first time I enjoyed talking to a native. This strange people seem to know no social distinctions; Smail, the son of peasants, might well be the son of a rajah. I made him sit down beside me; and I asked him about himself, and Rolain.

"What does he do in the jungle all alone?"

"He does nothing. He just looks about him. When I am with him he sometimes talks to me. But I think he mostly talks to the spirits. He is not afraid of spirits."

"Are you afraid of them?"

"There are many of them in the jungle," said Smail, in a very low tone; "more spirits than mosquitoes. There are some in every tree. I would not live here with any other Tuan."

He came up to me and touched my knee.

"The Tuan will pardon me if I ask him to tell the Tuan Rolain not to be always going into the jungle, and not to stay there so late. Look, the sky is yellow. . . ."

The whole jungle was bathed in golden light.

"That yellow awakens them. They are on the look-out. Their liver is acid, and they will harm anyone they find alone. . . . Ah, Tuan, my own liver is all melted. . . ."

* * * * *

Labels are for the ignorant and often serve only to mislead. A little peach tree, which for four years one has called Large Early Favourite, produces in the fifth year a crop of almonds or yellow plums. Merely a little incompetence on your part, or on the part of the grafter. Learning that the Malays were Mahommedans I had set sail for a sort of Algeria, but had landed in a Chinese city. Since my arrival I had lived in India. And suddenly I find myself in Polynesia.

The conversion of a people to a new religion does not modify the character of that people. It is a process of painting wood to look like wood. Man is incapable of abjuration. Beliefs are superimposed within him like coats of paint; they do not mix, and they are not effaced. The original colour remains and shews through. Christians are pagans white-washed with Judaism and Christianity. Theirs is a triple faith and they explain this anomaly by a mystery. They have a predilection for Christ, but they fear Jehovah in God the Father, and they have baptised the Great Pan under the name of the Holy Spirit. None the less, they have not learnt to love their enemies any better than the cave-men, but merely how to kill them more effectively. The Malays, too, have their three soul-coatings: animism, Hinduism, and Islam. They are obstinate Mussulmen, but quite unorthodox. Their invocations, that start and finish with the name of Allah, are really addressed to countless demons discredited by the Prophet. Allah is very merciful, and they do not fail to remind him of the fact every day. But a subordinate spirit has a narrower intelligence. He is also more sensitive to compliments. He does not disdain a few little offerings, but he is prompt to take offence. The Malay's life is passed in trying not to tread on the invisible toes of some irritable deity.

"Smail is a poet," Rolain sometimes used to say, "and he has too much imagination. But think what it would be like to live in a place infested by cholera, plague, and typhus, the germs of which were not merely noxious but cunning. How can a race that has always lived on the sea or in the jungle feel anything but defenceless?"

He described to me the denizens of this mythology as though he had seen them himself. The black Prince of the Genii, Sang Gala Rajah, who has preserved, almost unaltered, one of the appellations of Siva. Skin, blood, and bowels black, jaw with curving tusks like a boar, and limbs covered with bristling hair. Too powerful to be really harmful. He merely crushes inadvertently what happens to be in his path. His children are much more dangerous, —not from malice, but because they are interested in men. To take an interest in anyone is always to make him suffer. It is the thread a child ties to the beetle's leg. There are also spirits who do evil, and believe they are doing good, like the Spectre Huntsman, whose love for his wife drove him mad. She, being with child, wanted a male mouse-deer carrying its young in its belly. The desires of a woman are often absurd, but not more so than man's pretention to satisfy them. At first he killed nothing but mouse-deer. Vain massacre. He flung their carcases over the mountain tops and they were sometimes picked up, with their bones broken, in the valleys. Some of them had indeed a pouch in their bellies, but it contained only musk. He became saturated with musk, and sometimes by night the smell of him still drifts over the plains and troubles the minds of men. He has lived so long in the jungle that his thighs and his chest are covered with moss and orchids. Now he kills everything he sees. He bellows at his exhausted hounds as they range over the tree tops, belching forth miasmas and slavering poison.

Tupapaus from the depths of the Pacific, Pisasies from Dravidian India, Jins from Arabia, not to mention all the malignant dragons hawked along the coast by Chinese junks,—this is enough to madden a scattered population already beset by wild beasts and snakes and crocodiles. But the worst spirits are those born on the earth itself: neither Gods nor Genii,—wretched spirits who once were men. They are but the more inhuman. They have their own special grievances. Life, which deceived them, has made them like bees frustrated of their honey, a swarm of blind and wandering hatred. For, among all the peoples of the world, the living indeed complain of life, but only the dead are inconsolable.

Souls without bodies,—they exist perhaps, but they do not live. To live is to possess a body, and through it to possess others, or at least to have that happy illusion; to take a share in the eternal process of creation. . . . The rest is but a troubled twilit dream. The spirit, outside matter, gropes and is helpless. It desires pleasure or regrets it—and even pain, which is preferable to apathy. If we are not to despair of the dead and of ourselves, we must believe in reincarnation, in the resurrection of the flesh, in the sensual paradise of Allah. But we do not aspire to these promised delights, we merely resign ourselves to their enjoyment. We say "God has taken my poor grandmother," and we only call her poor since she has been taken. Pent in the soft pulp of his flesh, man can only imagine his stripped soul as a seed of vague desire that floats or falls.

While we were talking of these things, our conversation was accompanied by a furtive murmur of voices from Smail's room. It was a kind of chant, a long succession of answering canticles.

"Smail's brother has come to see him," said Rolain, "and there they are weltering in poetry. . . . Smail!"

The verse was finished calmly, fervently, and then the intonation of the voice changed and sounded as profane as a motor-horn outside a church after the hymn has stopped.

"Tuaaan!"

"Come along both of you, and bring the book of pantuns."

Smail entered, followed by his duplicate on rather a reduced scale: the same ease mingled with reserve, the same look of grave and set surprise, the same liquid eyes. The two came and squatted on the mat near us. Rolain turned the leaves of the brown volume.

"Here you are. This expressed what we were saying:

Asam kandis asam gelugur
ketiga dengan asam rembunia

Nyawa menanggis di-pintu kubur
hendak pulang k-dalam dunia.

"Can't understand a word," said I.

"The two first lines of a pantun," explained Rolain, "are only a preparation for the idea that is to develop in the succeeding ones. They create the atmosphere without the crudity of metaphor. Here are bitter-sweet fruits, plants with an acid savour. It is to introduce what follows, as a heart is offered after fruits and flowers, leaves and branches[1]:

The soul weeps at the gate of the tomb;
She so longs to come back to the world. . . .

"And again:

Nasi basi atas para
nasi masak dalam perahu

Puchat kaseh badan sengsara
hidop segan mati ta-mahu

"So short a poem needs to be read slowly as a still life should be looked at for a long while. Indeed it is a still life: stale rice left in a boat.

[1] Voici des fruits, des fleurs, des feuilles et des branches,
Et puis voici mon cœur, qui ne bat que pour vous . . .
VERLAINE

"We think of a voyage or of an adventure, of him who was in the boat, and cooked the rice, and was hungry at that time—and yet the food is left untouched, and we scent a drama. Or perhaps this white rice that no one wants is in itself symbolic. The two last lines reveal the *soul-state* of the picture:

> Lividness of love, tortured flesh,
> Life is insipid and death distasteful. . . .

"It is the expression of so deep a disillusion that no desire survives, not even the desire of death."

Smail had taken back the book and was reading; he appeared to choose the erotic pantuns—which most of them are—and his brother's eyes glittered with pleasure.

> *Kerengga di-dalam buloh*
> *serahi berisi ayer mawar*
>
> *Sampai hasrat di-dalam tuboh*
> *tuan sa-orang jadi penawar*

> Red ants in the hollow of a bamboo,
> Vessel filled with essence of roses . . .
>
> When lust is in my body
> Only my love can bring me appeasement

> *Akar kramat akar bertuah*
> *akar bertampak di-goa batu*
>
> *Nabi Muhammad berchintakan Allah*
> *di mana-lah tuan masa itu*

Sacred vine of the jungle, happy vine of the jungle,
thrusting its stem into the cleft of the rock. . . .

The prophet Mahomet loved Allah. . . .
but then, my beloved, you did not exist.

All poetry is untranslatable, but in the translation of a pantun it is not merely the rhythm, the rhyme, and the assonances that are lost. It is the play on words, the equivocations, the tenuous allusions, that constitute their special charm for the Malays. One must have lived a long while among them to catch the various connotations of each word beside its literal sense. They all know a large number of pantuns by heart and are constantly inventing new ones. Their conversation is full of these poetic insubstantial images. It is a game of leap-frog between the concrete and the abstract in which the players constantly change places, and our anxiety to translate clearly, breaking the impulse of ideas, produces merely a flat sense of verbal acrobatics. Word for word translation is the crassest betrayal.

The first pantuns had amused me like those puzzle drawings that have to be looked at from every side to find some hidden profiles in the contours of the obvious objects. But it was not long before I discerned beneath all their ingenuity, a very sure and very concentrated art. I was as surprised as if I had discovered these dissembled profiles in a Chardin or a Cézanne. The two little Malays laughed at my astonishment, and Rolain said:

"You have good eyes, and they see a long way when you aren't looking at a wall."

"It does not matter which way I turn," I said, "there is always a wall. We are in a five-sided tower. I use my senses as I can. It is not my fault if they are scrawled with absurdities, and obscenities. It is atavistic. . . ."

"Scrape the wall," said Rolain. "There is also firm ground under our feet, and a shifting sky up above. We use our senses, but only to serve our logic and our intuition. Then we, too, write and draw, as well as we can, and the record remains."

When I got up to go, it was beginning to rain. There were already stars in the sky, but a metal shutter clashed thunderously down like the shutter of a goldsmith's shop-window and barred them out: the palm trees clutched at their upturned umbrellas, and the scared array of leaves fled under the darkened colonnade of trees.

"Don't go away," said Rolain; "we'll dine together, all four of us. As for the night, the beds are here already; one has only to uncross one's legs and fall upon a cushion."

We ate rice and curry in Malay fashion, with our fingers,—but there were silver bowls in which to rinse them. I was as gay as a child having lunch in the train, at last allowed to gnaw a chicken leg. And as, to whet his delight, the child thinks of a stern grandfather before whom he has to behave, I thought of Potter. What would he think of this "native" dinner party?

"He would become aware of the fact that four gentlemen can eat with their fingers."

"He would be aware of nothing," I said, "but our degradation."

"Possibly. Potter is English, his moral code is simple: do as everyone else does. But if everyone acted like everyone else, no one would ever do anything. Without the anarchists, humanity would perish, or turn into an ant-hill. Organisation is the great danger. . . ."

"Do not talk French, Tuan; to-day we are your guests."

"He is right," said Rolain, "we spend our time in cavilling. Much better say like Smail, when he hears the rain: 'Chandrawasi is shedding his feathers.' He would sooner speak of the legendary bird although he knows it is the rain in the branches."

The rain had stopped its fusillade on the roof, and now only scattered a few salvoes as the gusts of wind rose and fell. In the intervals of silence, there came through the window, with the smell of damp leaves, a wailing cry like the call of a wounded creature.

"It is the Punggok who has seen the moon again. He always flies in the rays of the moon. He longs to be caught in her nets of white silk, and whirled up to her, but the meshes are too fragile. He falls to earth and moans."

The Punggok is the only night bird that is not of evil omen. Its love makes it innocuous. The others have a bad reputation: they lend their phosphorescent eyes to the blind souls of the dead.

"When I hear them swooping softly over my head," said Smail, "I fancy I hear Penanggal's entrails flap-flapping in the air."

"Brrr. . . . What's that story?"

"Tell us, Smail, the story of Penanggal," said Rolain, lowering the wick of the lamp which went out with little palpitating glow-worm flashes, "darkness is the proper light for a ghost story."

"The Penanggal was a bad woman, for she spent all her time at her window. She never thought of warming her husband's belly with white rice and spiced sauces, but only the bellies of the young men by shewing them her breasts, which were as round as bowls, and her eyes, which were as hot as pepper. One day she leaned out of the window to ogle someone. Her husband came and cried: "Look out! You will fall!" So, as she was *latah* . . ."

"*Latah?*"

"It is," said Rolain, "a sort of hysteria to which certain Malays are subject."

". . . As she was latah, she struck her chin so hard with her knee that she tore the skin of her neck, and up went her head in the air with the lungs, stomach, and entrails, all dangling like the billets on the necks of wandering buffaloes. Nothing was left to the husband but a sack of female skin."

"Many husbands would be quite content with that," observed Rolain.

But Ngah, Smail's brother, who had seen the Penanggal, did not think the story comic.

"I have seen her, Tuan. A head perched on a branch, watching me with amorous eyes. The intestines were hanging down beneath it. I heard a drip-drip in the leaves, and there was a reek like that of a heap of decayed elephants. I wanted to say an incantation, but my tongue was as dry as a cuttle bone. . . . I said it deep down in my liver. . . ."

"There are spirits," broke in Smail, "who are not afraid of incantations. Those with only a great head of fire, and a long twisting tail stretching out behind them,—just like tadpoles. They live in the swamps too. Suddenly, at night, they dash up to the top of the mountains. Nothing can stop them. If they but touch you, off you go with them."

"Perhaps it is the male Penanggal," suggested Ngah.

"It has the essentials of masculinity," said Rolain. "Besides, every male is a creature with no heart and no bowels."

That night I made the acquaintance of numerous demons. The Mati-Anak, a still-born child; the Langsuyar, dead in child birth; the Hantu Golek, that comes out of tombs, and leaps and rolls upon the ground, swathed in its shroud. . . . Smail left it to Rolain to name them, as he would have been afraid of attracting their attention. He talked in a low tone, lending the spirits he mimicked his own sinuous limbs and indiarubber face. Beside him, his brother, gasping as he sat, unconsciously reproduced his gestures and grimaces; and against the frame of the moon-flooded window I saw two agitated shadows, two menacing but frightened spectres.

"Are the souls of the dead always malignant?" I asked.

"Always."

"And yet if I were to die I should not, I think, wish anyone harm."

Smail shrugged his shoulders.

"The Tuan is not evil, but when dead, he would smell as evil as the rest."

"Then you believe that my soul would become a hideous demon flapping round my tomb?"

"Your soul is your soul, Tuan. It will go straight to hell. But there will be perhaps ten thousand demons round your tomb."

"But what are the demons doing there if they are not the souls of the dead?"

"The mouse-deer asks questions of the buffalo," said Smail. "The Tuan is subtle. I do not know."

I, on the contrary, had the impression of being the buffalo. Rolain came to my rescue.

"Smail's notions are vague. He embodies emanations as demons and is satisfied. But what are those emanations that he compares to the smell of carrion? They are born of decomposition of the 'ego'. The individual is only the vessel for a mixture called personality. When the glass is broken, the cocktail evaporates. The glass is thrown among the refuse, but the vapours trouble Smail's brain. What the Malays fear in the dead is their thoughts, their passions, their deeds, freed at last and self-existent, all that a human fate bequeaths to destiny."

"But what is there to be afraid of in all that?"

"Perhaps," said Rolain, "the intuition, that is at the base of all religions, of what these things imply: All desire is the denial of wisdom, all thought, of comprehension, all action, of repose."

* * * * *

Ah! the night is too dense. There is no space between its atoms. The darkness eddies in a thick swift tumult like the drumming of fevered blood in a man's veins.

The night is a living thing that engulfs me, in which I am dissolved. Is this I—this outstretched body? This strangely solid object that yet seems emptied, like armour of a bygone day? I contemplate it and hover around it.

What hovers is a whiff of dust that thinks as a swarm of bees vibrates. It can move with a single movement and is sustained by myriads of wings. Fragile cohesion of contradictory impulses and confused desires and unknown instincts. That swarm is I, and I am afraid of my own self.

I repeat "I", "I", until the word has no longer any sense, and then would seem to be reaching its true sense, outside reality.

The individual. . . .

The river, what is it? The course that one may see formalised and drawn on maps—or the water it contains? The course is but provisional; the water flows, evaporates, is replaced by water from clouds and springs; harmless today, perhaps tomorrow full of cholera. Nothing is more unlike than drops of water. But the river is always called Sanggor.

Am I a myriad drops of soul in a changing body, as illusory as a landscape?

I hear a gentle sound of breathing close beside me. Have I been asleep? Someone is sleeping here. . . . Where is he? Where were we all just now;—lost perhaps, commingled outside ourselves? When we do not dream in sleep, it is because we are in the realm of the Universal. Is that what Rolain was saying last night? But what he says is always . . . so tentative. . . .

But it was simple enough in old days. I was

myself. I had a body, a soul, a life. All very solid, broadside against the wind. Then I was told I should perhaps have several lives, and my moorings began to loosen. Now, I have a thousand souls, or more. I drift like a phantom ship in a fairy tale.

I want certitudes, even if they be as menacing as a roll of thunder.

The Catholics envisage hell without great perturbation. Anything is more comfortable than nothing.

If it was only either heads or tails. . . .

Certitude. . . . But certitude is ignorance. The ignorance of children. The child Newton shook the apple-tree to eat the apples that fell. They fall, and that is all. Why should we ask why? Since explanation only deepens the mystery? . . .

Rolain likes all this mystery. But it seethes in my head and makes me dizzy. Who was it said "I think, therefore I am?" I think, I think,—and the "therefore" is that I no longer know if I am. . . .

These Malays are interesting. So is the jungle. Trees, nothing but trees. A monotonous country. One enters it—I feel I am nearly asleep—and finds the enchanted forest. What new and vaster landscapes are ever opening out, as one advances! Yes, again, that river . . . My banks are no longer sheer and narrow, the water spreads and swirls, eddies and flows back. First traces of salt: a brackish, uneasy savour. The little fishes wonder how it will all end. . . . These comparisons are absurd. But they help me to get back to myself, or to lose myself entirely. After all, need I so dread the sea? . . .

III

THE JOURNEY

III

THE JOURNEY

I

A meeting of the Planters' Association of the Sungei Sanggor district will be held on Friday the 14th instant, at 10 a.m., at the Pengkalan Mabok Club.

Agenda:

1. Proposal for restriction (voluntary or compulsory) of the rubber output.

2. Reduction of the coolies' wages.

3. Hospital.

4. General.

Owing to the importance of the items on the Agenda, you are earnestly requested to attend this meeting.

Kupu-kupu terbang melintang
terbang di-laut di-ujong karang

Pasal apa berhati bimbang
dari dahulu sampai sekarang

"YOU don't want to go to this meeting?" said Rolain.

"I don't know. I came to ask you if I ought to go. It's very important, apparently.

You've seen the agenda. Government are to be asked to control the production of rubber. Well, perhaps that's the remedy—to produce less so as not to produce at a loss. But legislation will be necessary. Voluntary restriction would never work."

Rolain was picking out a Malay tune on a kind of little two-stringed viola. From time to time he glanced at me with a worried air.

"Hang it all, Rolain, tell me how you want me to vote, or go to the meeting yourself. It's your estate after all."

"I'll present you with it."

"Thank you for nothing."

The bank balance was gradually dwindling; and I knew that a good many of the coolies would soon have to be discharged.

"The situation is critical, I come to consult you, and all you can do is to make a stupid joke. I don't care a blast about your plantation."

"Then you're wrong," said Rolain. "I don't yet believe in over-production. It's only a preliminary crisis. I shouldn't trouble about their meeting. Things always come right in the end; in two or three years from now you'll be a rich man."

I suppressed the only word that came into my mind and went out.

The vertical sun poured like burning fluid from the tips of the motionless palm fronds. On the ground quivered a trellis-work of light and shadow; and in the air a shrill cicada squeaked like a pencil on a slate.

Give it me, would he? . . . And how could he live here long without going mad? The last time I came I raved throughout the night . . . . Those palms might be on show in a hot-house—especially the one with the crimson trunk. Who ever dreamt of such trees in France? It's winter over there; February. And good old smell of fog. . . .

Lured by the sound of a spring I went down into the ravine and stood without undressing under the falling water. Then I lay down in the sun, steaming like a horse. How I wished I could evaporate altogether! . . . And I fell asleep.

I felt a presence beside me and opened my eyes.

"Ngah!"

"Tuan."

"What are you doing there?"

"I want to talk to the Tuan."

"Well, go on."

He hesitated, then turned his head away:

"It does not matter . . ."

"You must not be afraid to talk to me, I shan't do you any harm."

"I know. I am afraid of white men but not of the Tuan."

"Why are you afraid of white men?"

"Their hearts are drunken," said Ngah; "and besides they drink alcohol."

Lowering his eyes, he added suddenly:

"I want to be the Tuan's Boy."

"I'm not a pleasant person to work for," I said; "besides I've got a boy already."

"He is only a Chinese."

Yes, only a Chinese, I thought; he is quite right.

"Very well, Ngah, I'll think it over. Go away now."

He got up, walked a few steps, and then turned to say in a tone full of meaning:

"*Ikan gantong, kuching tunggu.*"

I watched his lithe and silent figure disappear.

Here was another riddle for me to ponder; "the fish and the waiting cat". The fish? . . . I understand. I'm the fish. It is an allegory of a very great desire and a very little hope.

"Come back," cried Rolain; "You're sulking like a child.

"I think you need to confess yourself," he added, when I had lain down on a rug. "It is sometimes useful, although the confessor and the penitent never speak the same language. But the effort remains. The soul has plunged . . . Tell me first why you haven't come to see me for so long. You're dropping me."

"Dropping you, indeed! I like that. The plain fact was that I wanted to be alone. But one wants to be alone not to escape others but to escape oneself; and I thought the only way to do that was through meditation. Yes, but it needs courage to contemplate one's heart and one's body and detest them. I know quite well that the sole object of contemplating the navel is to cease to see it; but I should dispose of mine by hara-kiri before the first day was out. No, I was certainly intended for active life."

"Well, and what about the plantation?"

"Yes, I tried. I said to myself: You are lucky enough to be a rubber planter. Just think of what it would have meant to you when you were a schoolboy, with no certain prospect in life but soldiering! Well, I'm beginning to loathe that plantation. In the first place it's the wintering season. Winter, when the thermometer stands at 90 degrees; and the absurd trees all looking moribund, their trunks covered with canker and mould, their corrugated bark. . . . Black men who look like tormenting devils dash about among those trees and probe the wounds with little expert stabs. Poor trees, with their bare appealing arms! Come and see them —It's quite tragic, I assure you."

But Rolain smiled at these Dantesque visions.

"There's a comic side to it as well. For instance, the other night I got up to try and catch out the drying-shed watchman. I walked like a cat, with bare feet. I find the door ajar, cautiously insert my nose in the crack . . . There, point-blank, a pair of gleaming eyes. . . . Ah! What a start I got! And how he must have laughed. . . .

"Sometimes I wander round the cooly lines before dawn: I find it very instructive. The 'Pests and Diseases' Kangany sleeps in the unimpeachable Letchmy's room. I see shy shadows wavering behind the pillars. Things are happening. . . . Young Perumal, for instance, what is he doing in Mukkan's line? Well, I managed to meet him later on at work in his row of rubber trees. I had some fun in making his black skin blush. . . .

"One night the dogs were after me. A pack of four and three footed skeletons—most of them are lame—leapt out of the dark corners, and barked and barked until the sound of it made a sort of continuous tremolo . . . but you've heard it of course. Fortunately some of the men came to my rescue, and beat the brutes off with sticks and stones, and broke a few more legs I expect. . . ."

"Yes," said Rolain, "I can hear the modulation that it must have made in the tremolo, from shrill fury to shrill pain—from A sharp to B flat."

"Oh well—it wasn't so funny at the time."

"No. It reminds me of the old nursery book. *Sophie's misfortunes*. Go on."

"Well, I will pass over trivialities. I plunged into my work. I multiply the mileage of my zig-zag inspection of the estate, I walk up the big drain from its outlet—that's a job, I can tell you; mud up to the waist, and when you pull one leg out, the other sinks in . . . Then the factory, the office, correspondence, accounts —the usual pleasant little wind-up to the planter's day. But when I get back in the evening I feel as if I had done nothing. How dull one is, alone in the evening. . . ."

"But . . . Palaniai?"

"Palaniai? . . . A plaything, a statuette. Yes, she looks well against the white sheets; a small negative Venus. Well, when I see her coming, for all the world like a dog wagging its tail, shamefaced but full of self-conceit, Ah! I feel I could boot her out, the little beast! . . . After that you can imagine what happens when I try to get some information out of Joseph, and he turns his face to mine, black, flat and vacant as a slate. 'Beg pardon, sir?' You old cow-pat face! . . . Yes, that's what I said to the worthy creature yesterday.

"And Ha Hek! It's Ha Hek above all that riles me beyond endurance. He is so correct! And that Chinese smile, that eternal moon smile, compounded of servility, astuteness, and contempt. I have only thrown a roast chicken at that smile as yet,—I haven't got a revolver. You understand, it's his very existence rather than his faults that I can't forgive. I wouldn't so much mind the dollars that he finds lying about and slips under papers to see whether I shall miss them, and the pork with which he stuffs me in order to smuggle his opium. . . ."

"How do you mean?"

"Yes, when he goes to town he brings back tubes of opium concealed in pork; he knows very well that the Malay police, being good Moslems, won't touch it. But I suspect him of using other hiding places, not in pig's flesh. He sticks them all about his person. . . . And the way he irons my linen! Before he puts the iron on, I've seen him fill his cheeks with water and splutter it in a fine spray over my shirts. But worst of all, he strains my coffee through an old sock that must date from Stark's time. . . . But why tell you all this? I've really no grudge against anyone—except myself."

"Yes, tell me about yourself. Tell me what is at the back of your conscience."

"If that is what you want to know, I don't mind telling you I have found many blind, misshapen monsters in the depths within me. Unsuspected instincts. . . . That is what disgusted me with meditation. But must we stir up all this?"

"There are no monsters," said Rolain. "Have you ever seen an octopus breathe? It's like a lump of heaving gelatine. It may seem vile. And yet we gather together to eat. What a spectacle for an octopus! Let us look things in the face. The monsters of the great abysses do not astonish us for very long, they are too interesting. They are phosphorescent and can do without the sun, and they use such lights as they have to serve their appetites. We must do as they do when we search our souls."

"But what we find there," I said; "always looks a little dubious."

"Not dubious, but odd," corrected Rolain. "The fault is in our vision. We always look awry at what we see for the first time. But a frog-fish is just as innocent as a shark. You come up suffocated by the first plunge, but you will know nothing of the sea until you have done your twenty thousand leagues."

"That's discouraging."

"Not at all. The best voyages are long voyages, especially those whose goal is unknown. Life is a grand thing because it has neither head nor tail. We don't know whether we have begun to exist, nor whether we shall ever end, and this inclines us to die cheerfully."

"Rolain, I should like to believe that this life is but a stage and that it draws nearer to a goal. If we could see the forces and the faculties of man developing throughout his life, it would indeed be evident. But old age troubles me. Decrepitude, I mean . . ."

"Perhaps it is only weariness at the end of one stage of the journey."

"But in that case isn't it useless and even dangerous? The way we cling to life seems to imply that we have only one life at our disposal. Those who believe they will be born again ought to commit suicide at the culminating point of their existence."

"We never know when we have reached it," said Rolain. "We always see ourselves wiser than the day before, and inane old gentlemen are found lecturing their juniors. That proves nothing. Fatigue is a condition of training. But why always look at matters from the individual's point of view? It is hardly worth an individual's while to kill himself. He is no more than a fermentation that swells and bursts. The battle of the infusoria is without intrinsic interest. Let us but hope that the wine will be good."

"Yes," said I, "for the delectation of angels; I know that story. It's the doctrine of self-renunciation."

"But what more do you want? Merely a memory? Instinct is just such a memory, that only retains the essential. Are you sorry you can't remember your first feeding bottles? And yet, scarcely twenty years ago, they filled your life. Your deep desires of today, they too are but the gropings of childish fingers. Self-renunciation is not the suppression of desires and passions, it means a willingness to be reduced to elements, but at the same time to use our temporary cohesion; to obey our instincts with compliance and detachment; to liberate all our souls so that their encounter may be fruitful. The very word asceticism means exertion not atrophy."

"That morality is not for everyone."

"No morality is for everyone. I am talking to you. I can see what is torturing you—remorse."

"Remorse?"

"Yes, remorse for what you have not done, the only pitiless remorse. Your desire for action is merely vexation at the thought that you are marking time. But it is not physical activity that you want; have you not just admitted that you tired yourself in vain?"

"And yet I had dreamed of an adventurous life. The first time you talked to me about Malaya. . . ."

"Yes, you were out for adventure—and you were disappointed. Now you think you have exhausted Malaya. Nonsense. No country can be disappointing if you explore the depths of it. Satiety is a disease of the tourist. You must know how to turn over the page. The world, even the smallest corner of it, is a Book of the Thousand and One Nights, which means that it won't stop at a thousand, nor at a hundred thousand. . . . There will always be a unit to add to the infinite. Surely you must feel that you don't yet know Malaya."

"I know I don't," I said; "and that's perhaps just what has upset me. The other night when we were talking about the spirits of the dead, I suddenly saw the place as a mystery untouched, unfathomable. . . . And there was I, like a little bewildered insect. You spoke of satiety—it isn't that. It's more like terror. Conceive yourself loving someone for a long time, and suddenly seeing him or her in a new aspect. . . . You had not known nor really understood them. Then, instead of advancing further into that alien soul, you withdraw into your own. Yes, that's what has been the matter with me—now I know. I'm keen enough, but I'm frightened at what I find. I remember, when I watched the merry-go-rounds as a little boy, I could never make up my mind to get on them at first; I had to let them turn several times before I chose my horse; I wanted none but the finest. It was always the one which had just gone and it never returned. I hesitated and went off; good-bye, horses—horses not for me. Then suddenly from all that cavalcade I chose a pink rabbit, and almost died of shame when my little friends saw me on its back . . . But I'm talking nonsense!"

"Not really," said Rolain. "All great lovers are shy. Let the pink rabbit run away with you. He was the handsomest after all."

Smail came in with the tea. I caught sight of Ngah in the next room and called him. I had just made up my mind.

"Rolain, I am going to dismiss Ha Hek. Here is his successor."

"A very good idea. You can never know a country well except from the people it produces. In Malaya you must surround yourself with Malays."

He hesitated, lit a cigarette and went on:

"I say, this meeting of planters—it's very important. We mustn't miss it; we'll go together. And after that, we'll take a trip, no matter where, along the Eastern coast. I should like to show you the Eastern coast. . . . There—that's settled. Hi! Smail!"

Smail, who had just lifted a Malay kris from a large brass tray to make room for the tea-things, started violently. The kris slipped from his fingers and fell among the cups; the tray rang like a gong. Smail stood petrified, with haggard eyes fixed on Rolain. But Rolain said calmly:

"All right, Smail, I didn't do it on purpose. I only wanted to tell you to pack our luggage tomorrow for us to start on Friday. Wake up."

I had never yet seen open eyes awaken. Smail emerged from his trance.

"Excuse me, Tuan. . . . I am *latah*. There is a devil in my body."

He was pale and I thought he would have fallen. But Ngah had got up and helped him out of the room.

Rolain picked up the Kris.

"It's a fine kris," he said; "There's nothing remarkable about the sheath, but look at the curve of the hilt; it's like the curve of a human body, tense and ready for a leap. And the undulation of the blade, those five layers of welded steel. . . . It is believed to have belonged in days gone by to the famous Panglima Prang Semaun. Smail is always upset when he touches it. The poor lad's very nervous. . . . A fine thing isn't it—that flame of steel?"

"It's a bit rusty."

"Yes, the whole point is rusty. Bloodstains, apparently. Have you noticed that in this country rust does not dry and sometimes changes colour? When it turns red, the kris is said to be thirsty. . . . I've never seen it so red. . ."

II

Every year it was proposed that the club should be rebuilt. But this outlying district of mostly small plantations was not rich. When any funds were available a Chinese contractor pocketed them as payment on account and disappeared. When the price of rubber was down, no one paid his subscription, not to mention for his drinks. Chits were signed indefinitely. Suddenly the secretary, one Scarlet, took fright and posted up a black list of members who would be refused all drinks. Then the unfortunates stayed at home, waiting for better times. Some of them would arrange to meet at Scarlet's place, who, in spite of his resentment, could not but offer drinks to his debtors. One day, when they had been told that he was out, they had made his boy bring them drinks, and had serenaded him with tunes on his gramophone for hours together. Then, fired by cocktails, they invaded their host's room, dragged him out of the window and bore him in triumph round his own garden.

The club was housed in an ancient, and still

temporary, building, consisting of a bar and billiard-room combined, and a reading room. "Ladies" and "Gentlemen". But there were only two ladies in the district, who didn't hit it off together. From fear of clashing, they never turned up. Still, it was on their account that the *Vie Parisienne* was excluded from the reading room where the other illustrated papers were laid out on tables, and restricted to the bar; the journal was taken in on our account, from a feeling that the Frenchmen wanted something to remind them of *Gay Paree*. Certain members only looked at it when they were the first to arrive.

We were very late for the meeting, and yet we only found three planters, playing billiards. Each of them regularly missed his shot and said: Damn. It was monotonous. A few little toads were hopping about across the floor after insects. I watched them suddenly shoot out a tongue so long and thin that, when it slipped in again, it seemed to run right through them. After which they heaved and bloated in ecstatic hara-kiri. I waited in agony to see one of these toads explode under the huge feet of the players, but Rolain assured me that the toads were more skilful than their adversaries. "How wonderful to be a toad," he added; "nothing but a little lump of dirt, and from it emerges a note like a little white soul."

Little by little the club at last filled up. Old Holmwood, the president, appeared, looking careworn and wearing a necktie for the occasion.

There, too, was the formidable Bedrock, who could seize a cobra by the tail and crack it like a whip until its vertebrae were dislocated. He plunges about like a cyclone, blundering into all the furniture. For him the exterior world has no existence, he goes right through it. He exacts immediate and blind obedience. The other day in his car, noticing in the distance a small road on the left, he shouted to his driver: "Left!"; and the man swung round at once into the trackless jungle. So he turns up with the bridge of his nose skinned. Here, too, is his brother, shorter, heavier, and darker; like Bedrock's shadow at midday. Then the fair-haired Flowerpet, in baggy shorts displaying as he sat down, a vast expanse of fat thigh. A little to the side, on a deck chair, sat Shelford, a cigarette between his lips, a match-box in his left hand, and a match in his right. An attitude that helps him to be patient. He has decided he smokes too much, and is waiting until the half hour strikes. On the bar counter the sun helmets are piled up like a pagoda.

"Take your seats, gentlemen," said the president.

He had prepared his speech, but could not get it out. A costive discourse in the English manner. Three blurted words—er—and then two more. The company expressed approval in brief grunts.

Late arrivals took their places after a glance round the room, greeted by a succession of

"Hullos". Like a telephone room full of unnaturally placid operators. But when Stark arrived no one seemed to notice him. The president alone accorded him a wink. He, in his turn, affected to ignore the existence of Vellupillai the Tamil planter, who was sitting in a corner of the room and staring at us through his gold spectacles like a petrified owl.

From time to time someone signed to the Boy who made his way between the chairs, took the orders and returned to the bar to fill the glasses. The discussion soon grew animated.

"And now," said the president, "comes the question of increasing the hospital accommodation."

Protests.

"It's an official order. I venture to say that in present circumstances it is ill-timed. . . ."

And the Authorities come in for some hearty abuse.

"But we'll—er—give the job to—er—a Malay contractor."

And he added in a whisper, as though the Authorities were listening at the door:

"In that way we shall be left in peace for a long while."

He gained his point; he was greeted with a roar of laughter, the great English laughter that bursts forth suddenly, full-throated; it seems almost to have been learnt at school—like a laugh on a gramophone.

Then, they all began to talk at once. I noticed how unassuming, in a general conversation, seemed the French *je* compared with the Anglo-Saxon *I*. *Je* almost mute, blending with the words around it: the *I* isolated, strident, the only pronoun with the right to a capital.

"Yes," said Rolain; "but it's much worse with the Americans, who asseverate from the back of their noses with a lofty certitude.

Potter arrived just as the meeting was over. It was explained that a stiff resolution had been passed for transmission to the Colonial Secretary.

"Excellent," said Potter; "those old snails want waking up a bit. A government is always blocking the traffic. You'll see that restriction will come into force when it's no longer necessary, and will be suspended just when it's beginning to be useful."

This sally was applauded, and Potter himself was probably unaware of the wisdom of his words.

"Are you satisfied with my pupil Lescale?" he asked Rolain. "Yes, I put him through it, but it's done him good."

And he gave me a great clout on the shoulder.

"Only, he's a rubber-planter who has never planted rubber. That's a pity. It's just those little roots you put into the ground that bind your heart to the earth. Get that into your head, my lad. . . . And what about the Old Man of the Mountain? Not yet eaten by your jungle friends? I hear you live in a pile-dwelling on a mountain. Afraid of floods?"

"Yes," answered Rolain; "I can't do without mountains and pile-dwellings. They keep off quite a few men and snakes."

We were all standing round the bar. The Boy never stopped pouring out whisky; bottles of soda-water opened with a rhythmic hiss like ripples on the sand. The talk was, of course, of rubber.

"The trouble is to get the coolies to tap exactly to the right depth. It's a matter of a hundredth of an inch. I'm fed up with it."

"Nonsense," said Bedrock. "My method is quite effective and quite simple. I can't spare the time to inspect one cooly after another as if I were going round a bally museum. I don't so much as look at them, nor at the trees. . . ."

"Quite simple indeed, old Rocky-Ticky, Ha! Ha! Ha!" bellowed Potter.

"Hold on. I don't look at the cuts with a microscope. I go round the estate shouting and brandishing my rattan. When the date is an even number I shout: 'Too deep!' On odd days: 'Not deep enough!' The essential thing is that the idea of an exact depth should be hammered into the coolies' heads. My method is psychological."

At the other end of the bar they were discussing the ideal spacing of trees in a plantation.

"Oh those blasted Boards of Directors! One day it's close planting, the next wide, and in the end it's close planting that's right."

"Oh yes, until further orders . . ."

"You never know what to do."

"Well, I keep on at an average of twenty by twenty, a happy medium."

"Mighty clever," said Potter, "in that way you'll always be in trouble. Plant them thirty by ten, old chap. Then you can send in some nice photos taken either in one direction or the other, according to the fashion."

I caught sight of young Flow in a corner, blushing furiously as someone said to him: "You won't learn Tamil from books. What you want is a sleeping dictionary. You know what I mean?"

The club was getting boisterous. Some of the billiard players had hit on the idea of standing their glass of whisky and soda in the middle of the cloth to complicate the shots. Each time a glass was smashed, and the liquid poured in a bubbling stream across the green cloth, there was an explosion of mirth. The frantic secretary who tried to disarm the competitors, was beaten off with prods from billiard cues.

Rolain took my arm.

"Let's clear out."

The others tried to keep us.

"Going already? Off for a trip? To Pahang? Why that's a God forsaken place! Hi, stop them. . . ."

We started the car in an appalling tumult. Flowerpet pursued us with a toad that he wanted to put in one of our pockets.

"You're forgetting your barometer!"

From the village below rose a squeaky music, and the clash of cymbals; the gay music of a Chinese funeral.

III

Tujoh gunong sembilan lautan
kalau ta-mati sahaya turutkan

Potter, while cursing our levity, had agreed to come every week and cast a merciless eye over the plantation. "He deserves no credit for it," said Rolain. "He only enjoys what gives him an occasion for ill-humour." Anyhow, I could forget all my duties with a clear conscience.

A bad conscience gives a savour only to deception. I had no need of such an irritant. I was setting forth on a unique adventure with a friend who was also unique. I felt free, strong, at peace with myself and in love with everything. Mountains, sea, and jungle would have enough caresses to respond to my tingling desires. I brought them a heart grown young again.

And, indeed, as we crossed the first few hills, a new and unexpected Malaya was disclosed, and yet one that answered to the expectations of my heart; Malaya in her youth. We dipped down towards the rice fields. The rice field area gathers, without blending, an array of the tenderest greens, criss-crossed by neat little bunds, and dotted with islets of palms that set off the verdure. We were entering into spring. And it was Friday, the Malay Sunday. The fields were deserted, but along the edges of the roads the silk-veiled women passed in single file. At the entrance to the kampongs were little unguarded stalls of fruit from which it seemed the passers-by could help themselves. An idyllic scene. I recall a group of naked children round a guardian buffalo, pink, like a fat angel.

Then we began the ascent of those celestial heights that for hours had loomed ahead and now sank slowly to receive us. The rice fields disappeared and the jungle again encompassed us, but there too it was spring. In that jungle where the seasons seem to intermingle, where there are always budding leaves and dying leaves, where the trees do not agree and each follows the customs of its race, some baring themselves to the rain and the others to the sunshine, I was conscious, still, at that season of the year, of a more powerful afflux of new sap. The equatorial forest may at first seem monotonous, a flowerless mass of verdure. But climb up a little and on the stretching foliage below may be seen the pink haze of young shoots, the lovely efflorescences, preserved, as the Malays say, for the eye of God alone.

The road cut into the mountain side, then swept sharply up the hollow of a gorge. In those shadowed amphitheatres splashed by waterfalls, a carpet of green and black butterflies, with great fringed wings, rose up before us and unravelled into the darkness of the branches. Sometimes a long snake glided into the ravine like a thin cascade of oil. At every turn the air grew fresher and more vigorous. Rolain was driving, as I could not help raising my arms towards the drooping stalks of the bamboos, and the great arched fronds of the tree ferns. The car purred up the slopes.

At the top of the watershed a government rest-house serves as a shelter for travellers. There we were awaited by Smail and Ngah who had gone on the day before to get rooms for us. We were lucky enough to have the place to ourselves, and felt as at home as in the House of Palms. The boys had so harassed the cook-caretaker that he was expecting two royalties. A resplendent table had been prepared; all the government crockery and silver with the bull's head crest, the whole stock of bottles arrayed like skittles on the sideboard. There had been massacre in the fowl-run, and the kitchen garden had been swept bare; cocks, ducks, a sucking pig were laid before us, and European vegetables which the cook had grown, and six green strawberries—his pride. He applied to us for an increase of wages. . . .

But best and most unlooked-for of welcomes—tall flames were dancing in a fireplace. And against the white walls danced moths, dark moths with their dark shadows, fluttering with joy; and round the table, our two boys, silk clad, like butterflies of daylight. Isolated, like men in a light-house, we could hear the dim murmurs of the abysses. We went out to contemplate the darknesses that called to us. The pure fathomless night had absorbed the whole plain and its village constellations. The earth seemed to have shrunk; we were alone on a tiny vagrant planet.

When we came back we found our boys crouching cat-like before the fire. Smail was relating the adventures of Flea of the Forest, the astute little mouse-deer that tamed all the jungle folk. We gathered round the hearth dreaming of childhood evenings; and two children lulled us to sleep with grandmothers' tales.

* * * * *

As soon as we awoke, we climbed a rock above the bungalow and waited for the dawn. To stand upon a peak is a temptation to leap into the void. I thought of a lady-bird at the end of a finger, its little round back swelling with eagerness. Man's desire, or man's regret, is the angel. Oh to swoop down upon those soft vapours in the depths below. . . .

Behind us, the slope of the Straits, peaceful and set apart, between the sheer ridge of the peninsula and the dead volcanoes of Sumatra. Storms move across it in an atmosphere heavy with moisture. For months sometimes they shift and hover. The other slope foams like a sea stirred and swept by the monsoon from China.

"From here we can see our past and our future," said Rolain. "The coming weeks are here before us: the river that will bear us to those shores, those infinite shores—a white line edging an empty ocean."

We only saw the setting, I thought. . . . "How is it, Rolain, that though the body has eyes in front to see the way, our consciousness has its eyes behind? Fate carries us on the back seat of a cart, so that we only see things after they have passed, and the road speeds dizzily away beneath us. Humanity is an explorer who advances backwards."

"So long as we move," said Rolain; "there is no sense in asking whether we do so of set purpose. Whether life is action or observation. . . ."

"Ah, I recognise you there!" I cried; "the man of action who always looks as if he couldn't make up his mind."

"No, you are wrong. I never weigh the pros and cons. I let them settle their differences behind the scenes and take as long as they like; and in the end the conqueror emerges. But I know I can act more quickly than my thought can move. There are deeds that carry certainty. A man must be capable of the just and necessary deed, that will leave no regret whatever it may be."

He had said this slowly and with a sudden gravity.

"Rolain, there are such deeds in your past."

He did not answer. His averted eyes were fixed on the horizon. But what did they see? I should like to have looked close into his eyes and see what was there mirrored.

"Why do you never tell me . . . ?"

I noticed Rolain imperceptibly recoil, just as a bird that knows itself observed dips its head before it flies away. Mad hope to think that what the soul refuses may be betrayed in a man's eyes. He felt that I, too, had withdrawn into myself, regretting my half-implied reproach. He shrugged his shoulders.

"I don't like wasting time over the past. Life is a quest. Seek and ye shall not find. But to seek without hope, that is enough. There are some who think they have attained to Truth, and who are happy. The soft pillow of certitude. . . . I feel that in their place I should lose all interest in life."

The sun had risen from the horizon, and shot violet rays across the low, heavy clouds that would soon engulf it. All the jungle was awake.

"Don't you believe," went on Rolain, after a silence, "that when Wagner wrote "Forest Murmurs" he must have been transported in spirit to these mountains? In Europe the birds don't sing, they chirp. Here he had only to copy what he heard; to note down the pattern of bird-song against the vibration of the cicadas."

"And what do these birds say?"

"Birds only tell you what you wish to hear. Siegfried wanted to fight for a sleeping maiden;

in these days Siegfried would be prospecting for ore. You are out for adventure. . . . Listen. Perhaps it will be revealed to you."

The sun entered the cloud, and a great shadow gathered where we stood, moved down the slopes, reached the plain, and blotted it out. The jungle fell silent.

"Our future is dark," said I with a laugh, and then stopped with a vague feeling of superstitious awe.

"Yes," said Rolain in an altered tone, "there will be a storm in the valley."

But he was already looking elsewhere.

"Over there towards the North is the unexplored country of the Sakais who live in trees, and can deal death unseen from their blow-pipes—with their little noiseless poisoned arrows. But they are, in fact, pretty harmless; primitive people only want to be left alone. . . . Wouldn't you like to explore all that?"

I hesitated; my eyes ranged over that vast dark land, and I shook my head:

"No, I hardly think I would."

A cool breeze, rising from the shadows below, made me shiver. I got up.

Why had I talked like a coward? With him I knew I would go anywhere. . . .

"I often think," said Rolain, as we made our way back to the bungalow, "I often think of Teiresias. He was a man whose consciousness had eyes in front; he knew the future. He lived a life of marvels and adventure; he was man and woman in turn. He held that love contained more joys for woman than for man, because a woman gives herself more wholly, and because to be loved by a man is a thing more rare and more ravishing. He had looked on goddesses. But what are prodigies foreseen—what is a beauty that prevision has deflowered in advance? I imagine that his happiness lay in anticipation of increasing knowledge. He ended by knowing everything, even that he would die of drinking from a fountain. A fountain! A pure essence for the multitude becomes poison for the sage . . . I see him walking to the fountain, bending over it, and plunging his hands into that mortal liquid. . . . I understand him so well—lover of life—but worshipper of Fate. . . . "

That dream of all childhood, the impossible dream that a child tries to realise in his games at least, here it is in my very life. We are on a boat, gliding down the river at the foot of the mountains. I don't want to know its name. As a boy I used to say: Orinoco, Irrawaddy; but now the marvellous cadences of those names seem artificial. I want a nameless river in a limitless land. We shall twist and turn along that winding river—shall we ever reach the sea? I never grow tired of gazing, in a sort of blissful torpor, at the racing currents, the stir and ripple of the surface, the fascinating little whirlpools.

Our boat moves among much strange wreckage of the jungle in a broad uniform motion of the stream. The sun revolves around us. The banks slide past, new and yet unchanging. We keep close in at the bends to take advantage of the swifter current. Then the sky is darkened by a vault of virgin forest, above a tangle of lianas hung with great red fruit. Astonished monkeys, motionless, watch us pass, until a sudden thrill of terror scatters them among the branches. An azure king-fisher skims the shadowy shore.

Eight bronze men take turns at the oar and the boat-hook. Their task is easy; it is merely to keep us in the current, and to avoid projecting rocks and great trees floating downwards like ourselves, tangles of roots and branches torn up by floods or landslides. Islets of verdure, thickets of palms and creepers, when we try to pass them, suddenly swing round across our course and are swept against the bank. Sometimes a strong current surges out of deep backwaters and tips the boat sideways into the centre of the stream. Our Malays love these anxious moments. Lethargic where endurance is needed, they are stimulated by sudden peril. Then follow shouts and laughter, and sometimes a dive into the water after a lost pole and a sharp turn while the spluttering swimmer comes up to the surface. When the moment is past they doze again in the bottom of the boat, and roll their clove-scented tobacco in twists of pandanus leaves.

I watch them. They are placid, but easily excited. They look melancholy, especially the younger ones, and will laugh at a trifle. Aloof at first, they are now growing tamer. They understand that they are understood. Malays are polite because they are proud. Never give displeasure if you would never to be displeased. Shame is the only emotion that they cannot bear. Already I know them well enough to realise that the distrust of the first few days was not dislike. But I have yet to learn that a true Malay will sooner die than live with the memory of even an imagined affront.

* * * * *

Ngah, Smail's apprentice cook, is my professor of literature. He makes me read a whole book of old stories: The Adventures of Flea of the Forest, of Daddy Grasshopper. Then we go on to the proverbs and pantuns. They are more difficult; but I make rapid progress. I begin to follow the thread of what the Malays say when they talk to each other. What baffled me at first was the fact that I understood what they said to me, but as soon as they talked together all I could catch was a series of maddening inconsequences. Imagine, for example the following dialogue between two young Malays. The subject is a green coconut. What can they have to say on such a matter? Listen:

Osman, with downcast eyes, but with assurance:

"Where do the leeches come from?"

And he sighs.

Mat shakes his head reflectively:

"The hook is broken."

Osman protests:

"Would a lamp be lit?"

And Mat answers with a cruel laugh:

"The sugar-cane on the opposite bank is very sweet. . . ."

My reading gives me the key to this lunatic conversation. Here is the translation into modern dialogue.

The subject is a girl.

André, with downcast eyes, but with assurance:

"I've got a lech on that girl."

And he sighs.

Julien shakes his head reflectively.

"You'll have to whistle for it, old thing."

André protests:

"Then why does she make eyes at me?"

And Julien answers with a cruel laugh:

"So you don't see she's pulling your leg? . . ."

Here, indeed, are metaphors, but metaphors without life, mere phrases, the first expressions that came to mind, of origin unknown. In the Malay dialogue, on the other hand, all is allusion. It would be incomprehensible if one did not know the pantun of the leeches that come from the marshes into the rice fields; the pantun in which the sugar-cane of the other bank symbolises illusion or treachery; the pantuns of the hook and of the lamp. . . . Such a dialogue implies a literary training that seems amazing in a still primitive people. But can one speak of literature when a form of expression has become instinctive? The Malay recoils from any coarse exposure of his thoughts and feelings. The apparent preciosity is no more than modesty.

Sometimes, however, it is the desire to shine that transforms a general conversation into a match of wit, a poetic joust. They quote, they improvise. In these floral games old Pa Lawan, our head boatman, found only Smail who could hold out against him for long. The former shewed more erudition, the latter more imagination. The company fell into an ecstatic silence, then suddenly laughed and stamped their feet in a burst of excitement.

Out of courtesy, Smail always left the last word to his aged adversary, but he alone throughout the voyage was never surfeited with poetry. When evening came, as the moon waxed every day, a rising tide of lyricism flooded his soul. He knew nothing of the diffidence of our poets for whom the moon is an old and lawful spouse who may no longer be spoken of in verse. At the outset, the thin crescent was a nail-paring of Allah, and the demons of the night wanted to seize and use it in their spells against him—but Allah's shining finger-nail rent the darkness. Then it became the outline of a breast; a veiled woman bends down by night to light a little lamp, and in the dark house nothing is visible but that trembling arc; does she think that I shall shoot the arrow? . . . Soon the moon became a ripening banana, a lad who for the first time dreams what love may be. And when we reached the sea, Smail saw the full countenance of her whom he would wed. "Stop, for heaven's sake," said Rolain. "It's in all the Arab poems—you might well have spared us that." But Smail had only sung of the moon to conclude on this ancient metaphor, which to him was as inevitable as, to others, a nicely rounded tonic chord at the end of a melody. He stared at us, with open mouth and eyes. And I thought: "How happy are those peoples who find nothing stale!"

I had noted down a few of Smail's poems that I wanted to preserve; for he sometimes broke away entirely from his memories of oral tradition, and began to improvise—or had he composed them in the smoke of his kitchen as he watched the rice swell and splutter?—freer poems than the pantuns, to which old Pa Lawan listened with an air of scandalised appreciation. This revolutionary poetry upset all the metaphors. "*Mabok*—he is drunk," said Pa Lawan with a toss of his head, but he never failed to be present at these literary orgies.

Half way down the river villages were few. Sometimes, at the far end of a creek, or on the shore of a promontory, a few grey roofs came into view. We then put in to renew our stock of water and buy provisions. One evening we arrived at bathing time. A troupe of children were gambolling on a bamboo raft. Little waxen figurines, chubby buddhas with shaven heads and a lock of hair on the top of their skulls. As they fled at our approach, Smail hailed them.

"*Kulup! Kulup!*"

Kulup is a pleasant kindly word in Malay and always reassures shy children. It only applies to the very little ones, still uncircumcised, for kulup means foreskin.

"Kulup! Kulup!" and the children came back; and while they were tumbling round the raft like yellow ducklings Smail sang them a song:

Go, little children, go and bathe,
Cool your bodies warm as cakes,
Wash your bodies floured with dust,
Hide your naked bodies in the brackish water,
Naked as the buffalo that has lost its nose-ring,
Naked as the lizard with a top-knot on its head,
Your lock of hair has stuck to your heads—take care you do not drown,
The Archangel Jibrail would not know how to carry you.

Another time Smail had discovered from his Anglo-Malay calendar that the day following was to be a day of celebration for the white men. He thought we troubled about such things. Next day before dawn, while we were still lying in the stern under our awning of pandanus leaves, I heard a lively dispute. Smail was insisting on being put ashore in the jungle. "It is for the Tuan," he said in a suppressed but furious voice. So we lay up for a short time. Rolain was not awake. As I came out Smail was climbing on board laden with an armful of that lovely flowering creeper that droops from the tree-tops like a sheet of fire, swarming, however, with red ants, which he was hastily dusting off. Some of the others came to his help and were busy plucking the clinging little creatures from his skin, when Rolain too came out. At the sight of him Smail took the whole sheaf of flowers and flung them into the stream. He was weeping hysterically. "What's the matter?" asked Rolain. But Smail was already in his kitchen.

We saw only Ngah all day. To all our questions regarding his brother he replied in a firm, impassive tone: "He wants only to sleep." Rolain had made a few fruitless incursions into the kitchen. It was not until evening that I managed to console Smail.

"I wanted to put them on my Tuan's bed while he was asleep . . . for his birthday. . . . Why did those shouting idiots wake him up?"

He sobbed. Near him was a crumpled bit of paper; I picked it up.

"No," said Smail; "it's no good; it's too late. . . . I wanted to put that with the flowers."

I kept the paper after having shewn it privily to Rolain, and I remember the verses that were written on it under the design of two clasping hands:

My Tuan is great, his heart is before my eyes,
His eyes see what is above my head.

My Tuan is great, his wisdom is before my heart,
His heart sees what is beyond my eyes.

I could not reckon the time we took on our voyage down that river, on our passage through those solitudes. Gradually the green water clouded. Muddy tributaries from the tin-mine country tainted it with long trails of ochre. We scented China. It seems almost as if the Chinese take their Yellow River with them everywhere they go. Soon we were floating on an expanse of water that broadened and grew more slimy every day. It swelled and spread, overflowed the very foliage on the banks; then the sluggish currents once more began to move and the surface of the water fell, like milk taken off the fire. From it emerged a tangle of leaves, branches, stems, and a pile-work of stripped roots.

We now had to contend against the inflow of the tides. Our boatmen, buttressed on their long poles, their shoulders bent lower than their loins, thrust their way along the bulwarks of the boat from bow to stern; there they stood up, pulled out their poles, and went back once more. Pa Lawan explained to us that the tides are caused by the great crab that inhabits the navel of the seas. When he goes out to find his food, the waters plunge in a mighty whirlpool into the world below, and the sea subsides. When he comes back he stops the gap, and the water from the rivers raises the sea-level once again.

At last, by a narrow estuary, a sort of channel which the Malays call a "dead river", we arrived one day at a small harbour on the coast: an oasis of tall palms, a row of little hovels on piles, and a flotilla of canoes, as slim and graceful as gondolas, and painted in bright colours.

Beyond it lay the sea, flat, oily, a zone of deep purple and another of jade green; and, on the far horizon, three diaphanous islets that seemed to hover on the waves.

IV

Chabut Kekili

There was only a long hill to cross between our encampment on the beach and the little port. Or we could reach it over the rocks on the sea-shore.

The hill was covered with *lalang*, a tall and compact grass, intensely green. At the foot of the slope, under a few palms, stood an ancient fisherman's shelter built of lattice-work walls and roofed with *nipa* leaves; here we took up our quarters, without furniture, lying on the sand to sleep. We had indeed hung up our mosquito nets,— a useless precaution, for there were no mosquitoes. They served us as coverlets when the breeze freshened before the dawn. A canoe, brought from Kampong Nyor, complete with oars and fishing tackle, was propped against the back of the hut.

Every year the bay must have been hollowed out by the monsoon, and the long sleek dunes of sand thrown back further inland. Our hut still stood erect merely because it was half engulfed in sand. Of the more venturesome coconut trees there remained but a trunk aslant over the water, or a heavy pedestal of tangled roots. But the monsoon had now spent its effort, and the wrinkled sea gleamed languidly beneath the sunlight. It seemed to be alive only round the edges, like a mollusc softly feeling the jutting rocks, and the hollows of the beaches, with its liquid flesh.

From the very first evening we gave our lives up to the sea. It lay, a broad expanse under the moonless sky, black with a bordering of silver. But as our feet touched it they threw up sparks. The water was full of a phosphorescent dust, and so warm that as we plunged in it we merely felt our bodies growing lighter. I slid my hand over the polished undulations to watch them turn to silver like the nap of a velvet cushion. I got up, and from my shoulders fell streams of diamonds. Thus was I absorbed, when Rolain, who had gone ahead with the young Malays, called to me. As I swam after them, I saw my body enveloped in a halo, transfigured, radiant, the body of an angel. Effortless I moved as one floats in dreams, leaving a milky way behind me. Here and there, other seraphic beings drew nebulae from the void. If I were to die now, I thought, it would make no difference, I should still be swimming in a universe where millions of worlds are born and die. . . .

But that dense water, so charged with living atoms, was, by daylight, utterly translucent. One could see the grooved bed of the sea, and on it the surface wrinkles traced shifting filagrees, rainbow-hued, like wide-meshed moving nets of light. The eddying stars had melted into a blue effulgence that was still a sky in which I could imagine myself floating: aether, empty space.

At night, no sound but the ripples that crept slowly towards us, so near that we might have been lying on the waters, and the rustle of the sand as they receded. But the days were even more untroubled, more insubstantial. Under the vaultless sky, white void that flooded us with blazing light, all things became fluid. Dazzlement,—ecstasy. . . . We lived no longer in reality, hardly even in illusion, we were reabsorbed into light like this pallid world that dissolves in vapour, like the mirages that encompass us.

The loveliest dreams are those we dare not tell because they would be tedious. No one would understand the thrill they had for us, and we ourselves have forgotten them because the fibres that they touched were too deeply set.

We should never try to describe happiness. Those, the happiest days of my life, when we lived naked in the sunlight,—I fear to think of them too much, lest, in my memory, they fade. I do not even want to meet with others like them. They are, to me, like a divine apparition that leaves a man blind, and I believe that the visionary is he who has no longer need of light.

But I may tell of our childish sports. For we were as children whose life might be one long series of delights. We chased the swarms of tall crabs that circled like scythe-strokes under the palms and then, when nearly caught, shot off in the opposite direction. We went out fishing in our canoe with lines or nets. We discovered to what depth we had to lower the bait for every sort of fish. With one line twisted round the wrist and another round the great toe, we waited for the faint jerk; suddenly the line tautened and quivered, and we pulled strange marvels from the sea: multicoloured fish, speckled, gold-striped, spotted, prickly as rock-cod; and they were so lovely, so vivacious, so repulsive, that I could hardly bring myself to pick them up. There were some that squeaked when they were touched; others, dull of hue and wrinkled, that puffed themselves up in the hand like a balloon, and spat as they fixed you with a malignant eye. I remember a sort of ray, like a flat face with a small smiling mouth, that I put back in the sea because it looked so bewildered. Gradually the bottom of the boat was carpeted with a viscous mass, stirred by sudden tremors, as their iridescence faded.

Sometimes in the evening we went out harpoon fishing in a creek at the far end of the beach where a little stream flowed into the sea. The right time was the turn of the tide when the water came up to one's knees. Then, moving forward slowly with a torch in the left hand, one could see, gliding over the bottom as calmly as in an aquarium, huge crabs, long garfishes, and soles whose undulations faintly stir the sand. We had to aim low on account of the refraction, but we soon succeeded in stabbing at the right spot. We spread out and stalked our prey in silence. A sudden burst of cries and shouts for help, and all had to bear a hand in dragging from the water an enormous skate, bent like a bellying sail and darting its tail in all directions. "Hi! Tuan, look out," cried Ngah, "it is very poisonous; if you get stung you will be drunk for a week. . . ." At last we flung it on the beach, where it lay feebly flapping.

We observed the courting of the king-crabs. They emerge from the sea at dusk—rounded shields that appear to walk without legs, war-chariots advancing against the dunes. Then the stronger sex, the female, offers her back to some alluring male for a turn along the beach. Chaste delights, wrapped in a decent mystery. When you touch these odd creatures, they raise their edged triangular tails straight up in the air; and you may take hold and turn them over. The feet are then visible,—so many wriggling feet that it is hard to count them. I think there are twenty-two. And what an array of straps and flanges, hooks and radiators! . . . Impossible to disentangle the real organs in all this apparatus. What a contrast! The shell was so perfect in proportion and design, moulded and chiselled and complete. Lift the bonnet and behold the side dedicated to utility. No longer beautiful; amazing, and repulsive. "Ah," said Rolain; "you mustn't aspire to be an artist and a scientist as well. Could you love a transparent Venus? No, Venus has too many entrails. We would have her naked, her eyes closed, dead if possible, and changed into marble; then we can really love her. Let the poor king crab alone."

But the boys took it away for their supper.

* * * * *

One grows as easily accustomed to nakedness as to the most ridiculous garb, for in the last resort nothing is ridiculous except the fear of being so—such is our ape-like slavery to fashion. The first day I felt a little awkward, ill at ease, indecent. Malays can be naked in the sun; the sun is already under their skin. But beside them, in that light, we looked like plucked fowls. Rolain, burned by the suns of many years, was in some sort of keeping with his surroundings. As for me, I had tanned unevenly under my planter's clothes, which expose the chest, fore-arms, and knees, and lay a double thickness round the middle and a shade over the eyes. I emerged a variegated object, with every hue from white to brick-red laid in layers across my person: not unlike a croquet peg.

On the second day I was still feeling for pockets, but I was no longer shy of the palm-trees. The third day began the great roasting and in the salt water my skin burned like a mustard poultice. "Carry on," said Rolain; "your thighs are nicely done,—two fine loaves of country bread. Persevere." And one evening indeed, I emerged from my sea-bath as from a bath of hyposulphite: toned, fixed, indelible.

I observed that the colonial helmet was a European superstition; one can soon do without it; indeed we had grown used to going bare-headed on our voyage down the river. And I should certainly have preferred to die of sun-stroke rather than walk about the beach in the guise of a mushroom.

The absorption of so much heat and light through all the pores, which at first leaves only an impression of fatigue, is an infusion of strength: a beneficent exhaustion from which one emerges to live a fuller life. For the skin must breathe, drink, see, and hear. In Europe clothes take the place of skin, and sensations reach us through thicknesses of wool; we have the sensibility of sheep. Here the slightest breath, the faintest flicker, are received by all the senses at once. Nakedness brings kinship with the elements.

"The melancholy of Europe is not seen by those who have never left it," said Rolain; "nor by any who have not come back there after a long time away. It is a country in which I could no longer live; it is inhabited, not by human beings, but by marionettes. Utterly devoid of charm. There is nothing to admire but empty landscape. That, indeed, can be as moving as the jungle or the desert; but at the sight of a human being one must fly."

I thought of the feeling of wretchedness attached to garments, of which I had been especially conscious during the war. Those layers of clothes, those thick unwashed suits reeking of stale sweat, those buttons and straps. . . . I recalled a wounded man whom we had stripped to give him first aid, and who died in my arms; he looked more real, more living, than those around him. That soldier had become a man. He had, in a sense, been born.

V

Smail and Ngah were wrestling on the sand. Their skin, coated with salty moisture, shone like a fresh horse-chestnut. They were wrestling not to win or to impress the onlookers, but for the pure pleasure of the sport. It reminded me of books I had read many years before; Theocritus, the *Bucolica*, the divine *Dionysiaca* of Nonnus. O Dionysos! Ampelos! my truant companions. . . . I can still see the schoolroom in which I saw you then; on the walls of it were already painted the silken sea, the long crescent of banana-coloured beach. It is you who brought me here, and here I find you once again. For if dream sets the course of life, literature awakens the dream. We must never disown literature, our earliest nurse. Even among primitive peoples, she it is that opens the heart and eyes of man to what will be finest in his life. To become children once more, Rolain had said. But a child who has all the sea beaches in the world in his garden walks,—what would he do with this one? Use it as an autodrome for coconuts? The child who can imagine, cannot see. To enjoy the magic of the world one needs a more complex soul, and less innocent senses. . . .

"Have you noticed, Rolain, how colours grow more vivid when you look at things upside down? Lie at the edge of that sand-hill, turn your head backwards, and you will see two young gods on an enamelled plaque."

"Yes," said Rolain, "one ought to look at the world and oneself upside down. Everything then loses its reality and finds its truth. You can see at the same time the whole and the details, you can see that the sea is curved and does not stop at the horizon, you can see the sky in all its profundity, you can hear. . . ."

He stopped abruptly. Hear? . . . What could I hear? At first I thought it was the throbbing of the blood in my temples under the weight of that inexorable sun: a delicate, sharp pulsation that now seemed to rise out of the sea, a mechanical sound like that of a watch. . . . It was a long while since I had heard the sound that measures and delimits the universe—a watch on a table by the bed; sometimes it seems very far away, sometimes it swells into a hammer-beat that fills the ears, and one cannot sleep. . . . Or rather one cannot go to sleep again. For I had the impression less of an insomnia, than an awakening into an absurd but stabbing anxiety that takes shape before consciousness has had time to return. No, it was not an hallucination. My heart, too, began to throb: and I waited, motionless, for the inevitable. . . . And as we still lay in the same attitude, flat on our backs, looking at the sea and listening to that rhythm, we saw emerging, tongue-like, from the headland, an impossible, yet oddly insistent object, a new child's toy: a white launch with a white awning and a man in white standing on the deck and observing us through a pair of binoculars.

Rolain seized my arm, but too late to stop me. I had got up and tried to escape into the shadow of the palms. The launch swung round at once, headed straight at us, the engine slowed down, and she came neatly to a standstill at the foot of our *lalang* hill.

The man in white jumped ashore and walked towards us.

"My name is La Roque," said the stranger. "I am the District Officer."

"Sorry to meet you," growled Rolain, glaring at him, while I mechanically repeated his name.

He turned to me.

"Ah, you're French," he said in French. "I believe I was French myself some centuries ago, in the time when the French were polite. Tell that unmannered friend of yours that I shall not trouble his virgin sea for long."

He smiled to himself, hesitated, and then said:

"I must beg you to excuse my indecorous attire. But I will get into uniform."

And he took off all his clothes.

"There. I am not the District Officer. I am a man in need of a good swim. Will you permit me?"

He turned his back on us and walked down to the sea. He was young, tall, and thin, and he swam like a Malay. In a quarter of an hour he came back.

"Ha! Excellent. Bathing is the only good thing in this damned climate. Now lend me five minutes' sunshine, and as soon as I am dry I'll say good-bye."

"I was offensive," said Rolain, "but it's the best way of finding out with whom one has to deal. Pinch the dog's ear and you'll see if he squeals or bites."

"Perhaps you're still being offensive," said La Roque; "perhaps not. But good dogs don't bite happy people; only the unhappy ones. You're playing at Eden here and I don't want to disturb you. Besides I also know what politeness is. Do you know that in Java the natives have to sit down to talk to you, because a seated man needs more time to pull out a kris and come and stick it in your belly. That is politeness. The Dutch lay great stress on it. Personally I am English. . . ."

"Not very English though," said I.

"That's a very innocent remark! Every Englishman is very English. Any defect of race is made up by education, and vice versa. When I am married I shall regard your conduct here as shocking. An Eden without an Eve or a serpent is truly shocking."

Rolain, who had affected to ignore the conversation, here put in;

"It is you who are the serpent when you come and talk to us about morals. But we shall not taste the fruit of the Tree again."

How was it I had never realised that the fabled fruit, which contained the knowledge of good and evil, was morality? One always believes that a myth is incomprehensible. But no definition could be clearer.

"But why," I asked, "find fault with men for distinguishing between good and evil."

"Because everything thus becomes suspect. Tell a European that we have lived naked in the sunshine, and see what he says; but transport Smail to the Folies Bergère, and he will believe himself in paradise. Who is right?"

"Oh I know very well that one can be in paradise among people who are in hell. . . ."

"Yes, and he by whom the scandal comes is he who is scandalised."

"And yet the Malays have a moral sense; they, too, talk of hell. . . ."

"They keep it for us."

"I often have occasion to sit in judgment on Malays," said La Roque. "It is very difficult to condemn them. They are never guilty. When they kill their father and their mother, it is due to their terrible ill-luck. . . . And yet they have many faults."

On this point I did not agree with him, and was glad to quote the remark of Father Lebouvier, the missionary at Kuala Paya; "We have all the mortal sins except idleness. The Malays have none but idleness."

"It is their virtue," said Rolain. "If they were not lazy, they would not be so merry, vivacious, lewd, fantastic, and arcadian. It is not for us, who come of accursed races, to judge them."

"Accursed? For what sin?"

"Let us not dissociate sin and punishment. The sin-punishment was leaving Eden. Every land in which a man cannot live naked all the year round is condemned to work and war and morality."

La Roque reached across the sand for his coat and pulled out a note-book.

"That's not bad. I'll make a note of it for use when I get back to Europe."

"When you get back to Europe, you will see none but harassed people, all mistrustful, always on their guard, thinking only of defending their right to get the best place first. How can they possibly be happy? . . . And with it all, drilled like performing dogs."

"I observe," said La Roque, "that humanity is returning to its cradle. There are now a great many Europeans in the tropics."

"Yes, cursing their ill-luck all the time," said Rolain. "Departure from paradise is irreparable. We have become acclimatised elsewhere; that is to say we take a bad climate for a good one, and everything is upside down. And if you go back to paradise after centuries elsewhere you will find an angel of fire waiting for you in the shape of prickly heat."

La Roque smiled.

"Well, that's better than the elephantiasis reserved for your inhabitants of Eden. . . ."

"He takes everything literally," said Rolain contemptuously: "I mean by prickly heat that itching sensation that makes one feel so wretched when there is nothing the matter. Elephantiasis is not half so bad."

La Roque picked up his clothes.

"Your friend is very fierce. He is angry because he did not want to talk to me and he could not help himself."

"We came here in search of solitude," I said, and stopped short, thinking that this conciliatory tone might annoy Rolain.

"But you've taken the best place on my coast, you must put up with a visit from the proprietor. *A la guerre comme à la guerre, Monsieur*, and we were in it together."

"The great thing about the war was," said Rolain; "that nobody was a damned Monsieur any more."

We were suddenly aware of a tumult of cries and laughter. Round the launch which Smail and Ngah had been at first respectfully investigating, a naval battle was taking place. The crew had made a sortie; one of the marauders was being pursued under the keel, the other was boarding the vessel.

"Look at your confounded piratical Malays," said La Roque. "They've captured my fleet. It's time I went back and threw them into the sea."

I got up to go with him.

"I like the French," he confided to me as we got to the foot of the hill "They are people without opinions who always argue as if they had some. I've got some whisky on board."

We were greeted by barks from a shaggy terrier which, torn between joy and indignation, wagged his tail at his master and snarled at the stranger. We went down into a cabin glittering with enamel and brass, and I suddenly felt horribly ill at ease, like a man in dream who finds himself naked in a drawing-room. La Roque, in his formal clothes, had changed back into the Administrator of the District. He surveyed me with indulgence.

"So you're looking for solitude. . . . You don't know what it is, young man. If your friend wasn't with you, would you stay very long on that beach?"

"I should like to think so," I answered. "Anyhow he would stay there by himself."

He poured out the whisky, then the soda, and passed me my glass.

"A *s'tengah*[1] of civilisation. . . ."

It was iced, delightful, devilish.

A Malay boy came and stood by the table filling the glasses as soon as they were emptied.

"The solitary," explained La Roque, "has the soul of a criminal. He is a dangerous creature. I have done a good deal of shooting in these parts, and I know what I am talking about. The elephant, the seladang, the wild boar—when they live alone, then you have to look out. They chew their hatred . . . and suddenly they charge. . . ."

* * * * *

"I rather think I like that Englishman, Rolain. He might have been much more disagreeable. And that wasn't a bad retort of his about elephantiasis. . . . I say, tell me why elephantiasis is a disease of paradise."

"You're drunk," answered Rolain.

"Drunk or no, I feel very clear-headed. Is elephantiasis a good or a bad thing?"

[1] S'tengah; Malay for half-measure.

"Ah! The problem of evil," sighed Rolain. "What a bore! Let us keep off that."

"Yes, but answer me first."

"Smail explained it to me one day: 'When I tell the Tuan the story of Rajah Alang, the Tuan wants Rajah Alang to be happy. But then there would not be any story.'

"But what's the use of the story?"

"What's the use of creation? I haven't an idea. But creation implies evil. In Unity there is no place for contraries. But with plurality, differentiation, you at once get the more and the less good and all the gradations from good to evil. And there you are."

"In the last resort, all is good," he went on after a silence. "I don't complain of living in my own little skin—I find it very interesting. I like learning by degrees. . . . Time is a fine invention, isn't it? But God will have to reabsorb his own creation."

I remembered that Rolain had said to me one day: "Creation will never be finished, since time is an illusion". But I had given up looking for contradictions in his remarks. For him, to think was to contradict oneself: those whose minds are at peace do not think. A little wisdom may be won by the concoction of wild hypotheses, and fixed ideas should be left to fools.

"What are you thinking about?" said Rolain. "We were happy here, too happy to think of argument. Why have we been disturbed? I feel sure the charm is broken. . . ."

"Nonsense," said I; "it's all over. We are alone. How soft this sand is. . . ."

I rolled down the slope of the dunes. Baths of sand and sun were joys that never deceived; they strengthened and did not exhaust. How delightful to lie and luxuriate in that burning and resilient powder; to close one's eyes so sated with forms and colours, and see nothing but the shadowed gleams that slip through the eyelids. The sand is soft, the sand is sweet, like the body of the beloved in one's arms. . . . When I opened my eyes—perhaps I had been asleep—the sea was mauve. I ran down and leapt into it like a man who leaps to drown. I felt I must take from the lovely evening all that it could give. Rolain and the little Malays had followed me, and we danced in the water, and let ourselves slide into its slumberous depths. . . .

The sleek milky sheet of ocean darkened, and changed, as on other nights, into a black starred expanse. But between sea and sky, that ribbon of darkness, the earth, dark domain of evil, was also lit that evening, with phosphorescence. The bushes were full of fire-flies that flashed and went out in a sort of slow pulsation.

"Look, Rolain, the earth is lit to welcome us. You are right. All is good. Evil is a figment. Men are as innocent as those fire-flies. . . ."

The course of events seems, when looked at afterwards, to consist of a rigid concatenation of fortuitous causes. I owe my existence perhaps to the length of Cleopatra's nose, but in a more explicit manner to the length of all the noses that have contributed to form mine, and, allowing four generations to a century and two progenitors for each individual, I reckon more than two millions of them since Francis I. I dare not push my calculations further, for if I went back to the cave epoch I should see the billions of Cros-Magnons of whom I am the direct issue, and beyond them an earthly paradise so crammed with Adams and Eves that it must have been a perfect hell.

The creation of me called for a miraculous conjunction of chances: the dreadful hazard of conception that gave life to each of my forbears and more hazards that preserved them until maturity. One microbe more, and I should not have been born. Another, more alien than a brother would have come into existence, who, in virtue of that microbe, would lack half my genealogy, half the cells in my brain, but would possibly possess, in their place, the seed of genius or of crime. However, I was born, and, such as I am, I cannot believe that I am swayed by chance alone. I admit that if Rolain had not lost his way in the trenches I should never have known Malaya. And yet I should never have stayed in France, scribbling in an office. Africa, Asia already called to me. And perhaps in the Congo or in Cambodia I should have led the same type of life. Events give life its form, but personality its colour.

The interest of life lies in the struggle which we carry on, or think we do, against ourselves and in our own favour. To conquer, to surpass ourselves; to add dumb-bells to our weight that we may jump the higher. Those incapable of action are often fond of games of patience because they find in them the illusion of a close-up fight with destiny. For them, patience has more attraction that a chess problem: it is fatality alone they want to conquer, and they think they have done so when the game has been successful; wrongly, since the issue was fatal. Only by making a mistake could they have tricked fate. Men of action prefer the chess problem in which the player has to contend with the ingenuity of an expert, where victory is always possible and never delusive.

It is preferable that we should not know if our destiny is really the work of our own hands. Irresponsible, we should lack fire: responsible, we should agonise with remorse. No religion dares to rescue us from this uncertainty. The precepts of the prophet are added to the inexorable Mektub, and Grace to Free Will; we have no right to accuse God.

Man has a sporting spirit, and adapts himself to this journey through the darkness. He does not even ask whether it is fair that birth should offer each man unequal chances, like a gymkhana in which one competitor drives an ostrich and the other a guinea-pig. No one dreams of disavowing his personality. But the fact that life, like a goose-game board, is strewn with snares, and the death's head awaits you not merely towards the end of the game but on any and every square, seems iniquitous, illogical, even diabolic; certainly fraudulent. It was hardly worth our while trying to form our soul since it is often but roughly modelled at the call of death. Thus the novelists, creators of souls whose pre-existence or after-life is not taken into account, are chary of accidents. They only drop the most indispensable tiles on their characters' heads. But in life it is accident that rules the plot. One may say that each destiny is a series of tardy accidents with the decisive blow at the end.

And yet accident, though it binds, does not enslave us; it is lucky or disastrous according to our reaction to it. It is a problem put before us, a problem with various solutions that will take shape as events. Events are advents—accident made flesh and entering the human domain.

I am reluctant to cavil at causes, contingencies, the why and wherefore of events. Rolain would think it foolish, he who never wasted time over the past. I can hear him say; "Enough of this lyric peevishness." But would he see anything but folly in all I write in memory of him? If I have let years pass before I dared to speak of him, it is because I feared to destroy him in bringing him forth out of my heart. Then I realised that he was actually dying there, that little by little I was incorporating my ego in his. He used to say that two friends who part never meet again, for each of them has evolved according to his own personality and believes that the other alone has changed. The realisation of a character is called deterioriation. We refuse to understand what we had been too blind to foresee. If friendship is renewed it is with a new being who usurps a phantom's name. May Rolain, in my memory, never become a phantom. Perhaps there is still time to trace his likeness without overmuch distortion. Even now he would not recognize himself, and I must be content for him to live in these pages for me alone,—for me who can read between the lines. But in ten years what should I have made of him? A pedant, a prophet, an idol carved of wood. . . .

The intrusion of La Roque into our sacred solitude is one of those tardy accidents of which I spoke. A wisp of white cloud in the empty sky and tomorrow the whole heaven will be black. Thus had this white man troubled our atmosphere. "The charm is broken," Rolain had said. And I too had quickly understood that summons to reality, the cold comment of the little watch that tells us that we are but dreaming. On the morrow we were wandering about the beach, purposeless. Purposeless! As if the aim of life was not to do nothing! . . . And when we saw our boys, oblivious of the morning bathe, pulling all their garments out of their boxes and attitudinising in them like mannequins, we exchanged a look of helpless consternation.

VI

Laksana buah kepayang
Di-makan mabok di-buang sayang.

"O Tuan, there is a great festival this evening at Kampong Nyor. The youngest son of Rajah Long the *penghulu*, is to be circumcised. Many musicians will be there and even dancing girls from Johore, the real dancing girls belonging to the Sultan! The men of the white boat told us so. That is why the Tuan-Company came."

Smail said Tuan-*Company*, because the British Empire, for the Malays, is still the old East India Company. He added:

"But if our Tuans do not want to come, it does not matter; we will not go."

I glanced at Rolain, expecting a refusal, but he shrugged his shoulders with an air of boredom:

"As you like."

I picked up a cuttle bone and threw it in the air.

"Hard side up, we'll go."

It fell soft side up.

"You should not do that, Tuan," said Smail. "You should only question the spirits on a matter of life and death."

"Ah? Too late. They've said No. . . . Well, since it isn't a question of life and death, we'll go. Heads or tails is an excellent opportunity to prove the freedom of the will."

I flung the cuttle bone back into the sea. It fell the same side up, and floated for a moment. I wanted to see it sink. It reminded me of a little white launch. . . .

* * * * *

At Kampong Nyor, behind the old Malay village, there is a new quarter in which the younger civilisation displays its wares; a single street between two rows of blue-painted Chinese shops with long vertical signs printed in red on black. At the end of the street a large cleared space is reserved by Government for the *padang* or sports ground, round which are to be built the club, the school, and the police station. There football will be played, and *sepak raga* is already played with a ball of plaited rattan.

Though we only wanted to see the end of the festival, we arrived in fact before it had begun. The Malays admit divisions in the day,—hours that are, indeed, elastic,—but for them the night is just the night. At the edge of the *padang* opposite Rajah Long's new house, a low platform had been set up, and hung with a profusion of Japanese lanterns; though the only lamp as yet alight was the moon. A few vaguely expectant figures were crouching here and there, and in the kampongs little lights flashed and went out, little wandering gleams announced mysterious preparations. But of a festival there seemed not the smallest prospect. We sat down on a bank at the edge of the road.

"It is," said Rolain, "a potential, an immaterial festival that exists in space and eternity. Isn't that enough for you? Let us go and sleep under the stars. . . ."

But I was anxious to see the dances. I wanted to add to my collection of Malayan impressions. One day, at Singapore, I had seen a theatrical performance of the *Wayang Kassim.* They were playing a musical version of *Othello.* The Moor and his rival fought a duel, first turning three times round, and then, at the third turn, coming to grips. Desdemona returned from taking the air, pursued by her Chinese rickshaw man, who cursed and spat with great heartiness until the arrival of a scarlet-faced English policeman who put him to rout. "What have you done with the handkerchief I gave you?" said Othello, turning up his great black moustache with both his hands. "Ah! Tuan-ku," sighed Desdemona, "it is at the *dhoby's.*"[1] Othello killed her, but she came to life again at the end of the play, and the *dhoby,* a corpulent personage daubed with black and talking with a strong Tamil accent, appeared with the handkerchief. The only virtue in the whole thing was the burlesque, for the Malays have the gift of comic imitation, but it was not enough to give me a high conception of their drama. Today I was going to see dances,

[1] Dhoby: washerman.

and I expected a troupe of bayaderes in the Cambodian style. And perhaps, among them, there would be one, plump or slender, with a face like a full moon. . . . Before dawn came I would lead her, still warm from the dance, into the thick *lalang* yonder. . . .

"Under these stars of yours, Rolain, I look for a real, palpable, sensual entertainment, here and now. I have time to sleep. In forty years I want to remember this night as I sit drowsily by a great fireplace full of shooting stars. . . ."

Meanwhile Ngah, who was afraid we might get bored, had gone to buy some durians, and came back armed with a heavy chopper to open them. The air reeked with their smell, that always recalls my arrival at Singapore: a thick, warm, yellow odour, hanging in the laden air, that might come from the earth or the throng of tawny humanity on the quay. But for those who have learned to like them, those strange and repulsive fruits have a potent charm; the last always seems the best, and the next will be even more delicious. The taste of them is, in fact, so complex that it eludes definition: neither sweet nor sour, but rich and luscious and heady,—a vegetable cocktail. Ngah split the prickly shells and handed us the soft and sticky dumplings of cream-coloured pulp. The big oval seeds, as smooth as jungle-fowls' eggs, we threw out on to the road.

"Wait," said Ngah.

And he brought us some green coconuts. He slashed off the rind with his chopper down to the still soft shell which split with a faint crack. We drank out of them as though they had been gourds, and, after the durians, it was refreshing to feel that moist rough fibre against one's lips, and the milk, with its virginal taste of unripe almonds, sliding over the tongue.

A crowd had gradually gathered and the lanterns were at last lit. As we were making towards our seats, the door of the *penghulu's* house opened, and we saw him come down, followed by several women. They passed slowly along the road quite near to us. The women were holding brightly coloured veils before their faces. But suddenly Smail, who was beside me, gave a start: one of them had lowered her veil and revealed a little rounded face, pale yellow like a granadilla, and as she moved away, swaying faintly as she walked, Smail, motionless, followed her with his eyes.

"Haha, Smail," I said; "*puteh-kuning*, eh?"

Puteh-kuning means white-yellow, and is the equivalent in the Malay ideal of beauty, of our lily and rose complexion. But Smail, with the detached air that he knew how to assume when replying to an indiscretion, said:

"People pass, one has eyes, one sees them. . . ."

"Come along," said La Roque; "I have had seats put for the three of us in the front row beside Rajah Long."

He made the introductions. I had an awkward Sunday sort of feeling in my stiff white suit. Rajah Long, a corpulent and sulky-looking personage, shook hands and then carried his own hand to his heart, in Malay fashion.

A table was brought and placed in front of us, and we were offered large glasses filled to the brim with tepid beer. La Roque, who was already rather cheerful, talked incessantly. From time to time he turned to Rajah Long who answered with a forced smile.

"He's an old badger, but he has influence. I take care not to rub him up the wrong way. One has to talk to him in the old pompous Court Malay, which is very difficult, but he likes it. . . . I put down a lot of whisky this afternoon before the circumcision. A disgusting business! They do it with a splinter of bamboo,—it positively sets one's teeth on edge—and then they stick on a beastly mixture of clay, soot, yolk of egg, coconut fibre, with lots of prayers thrown in. Baby vivisection, I call it, and I tell you it wants some nerve to watch it. . . . Have you seen my new road? You know that since this week we're connected with the west coast? There will be a weekly service of autocars to Kuala Paya. The rest-house is nearly finished—yes, it's over yonder behind my fat Rajah's house. Civilisation on the march, what?"

I remembered having seen that road, from the top of the mountains. Straight, at first, over the plain, then winding—the whip of Europe laid across a new country.

"And, here are the famous dancers."

"Good God! How hideous," I cried.

There were only two, who might well have been chosen as contrasting extremes. Thin and fat. Two caricatures of the most accentuated Malay types. The thin one, bent as though with age, had receding shoulders, and a black, or dirty, skin. The fat one looked like a pallid frog. Both of them loaded with necklaces and rings. They swayed on to the stage, balancing their hands behind them. And as if to complete their grotesque appearance, they wore high heeled black leather boots. Rolain jeered at my disillusion.

"Now, what about your animal instincts?" said he. "But cheer up, my lad. Beauty is nothing but a mask. I guess the fat one has a beautiful soul. . . ."

"No thank you. Rather my Palaniai without a soul than the most beautiful soul in a lump like that."

The orchestra struck up an Arab air, one of those interminable repetitive melodies that seem so simple and are utterly elusive. All they leave in the mind is a recollection of bewilderment. Just as we invent tunes to the rhythm of a train, the same musical phrase constantly repeated sets us adrift. I no longer watched those ugly dancers, I voyaged in my thoughts.

I have often wondered whether the mechanism of my thoughts was the same as that of other men. The timidity of the adolescent is not due to the fear of self-revelation, but, on the contrary, to the fact that he believes himself a mystery and a discreditable mystery. Self-reliance comes when he sees that what he dare not confess is not abnormal, and that human speech is merely reticence. My most secret meditation is everybody's secret. But all do not exploit this common spiritual stock with the same methods. Some books reveal interior monologues that display it unadorned. Personally, I polish my reflections. For my own sole pleasure,—a precarious pleasure, like that of love. My self-posturings are like love's ecstasy and end in a similar disgust.

A lovely soul, a lovely body, fused even in a single being, how can that satisfy me?—I asked myself. Desire is always trustful and is always betrayed. Palaniai . . . I remember one day. . . . That ray of sunlight in the centre of her forehead; it made a tiny glowing moon that I eclipsed by bending over her. Even whiteness can be a stain. On that face, so delicately shadowed in its darkness, would a patch of lighter colour, a milk stain, like a wine-stain on a white woman's face, fill me with aversion for her whole body? . . . Why do we want to possess what is perfect? Is wine really less good in a cup because it is lovelier in crystal?

Still, you were lovely, Palaniai. But beauty, like all things, is a pretext. I used to look at you until I reeled with desire, and then I shut my eyes,—yes, so as not to see you as you are. The perfection that we seek only comes to us, like an electric fluid, in flashes. A continuous current would kill us. But those more subtle contacts —a waft of perfume, a strange glance that thrills us, the inexplicable rapture that we know only in our dreams . . . Ah! Must we always awaken? . . .

"The animal instincts, Rolain, are no great matter. One may well satisfy them since one is not thereby satisfied. The destruction of desire by sating or stifling it is always a quest of happiness. But I begin to be convinced that what is best in life is regret. The happiest man is possibly the ascetic, provided that he has kept his regrets."

"You are very young to say that. But regret, too, must be mastered."

Rolain himself is too young for what he professes. He is like me; face to face with life, at once an enthusiast and an unbeliever. . . . The heart of man is possessed by two devils, the devil that says, Yes, and the devil that says, No; the accelerator and the brake; and what we conceive as happiness is no more than the predominance of one of them. Hedonists and mystics are happy, who know what they desire, or desire they know not what. But in me these two demons are of equal power and they tear my heart. I love them and I fear them, and perhaps it is the one that frees me that I fear, while I love the one that has me by the throat. My life is a secret enthusiasm. But Rolain knows that, and for that reason he tolerates my company as a reflection of his solitude. . . .

A sudden halt in the music in the middle of an arabesque, awakened me. Such music is like a ribbon that can be cut no matter where. It has never exhausted its significance and no decisive chord kills it. Its cadences still fill the silence and vibrate in the souls of those who heard it; soon, too, their bodies will respond to the lure of that noiseless rhythm.

La Roque took advantage of the pause to resume the conversation.

"A Malay dancing girl," he observed, "is never beautiful, for then she would not dance. She does not take up dancing until she has lost all hope of marriage, or her reputation has no more to lose. And yet look at my good villagers: their eyes are shining, they're in love already."

"Love?" said Rolain. "Where do you see any love here? I hate the European mania of confusing love and lechery."

"It's just a manner of speaking. . . ."

"It's a manner of speaking that exposes the baseness of the soul," said Rolain, turning to me. "Among Christian peoples there is only one subject of conversation: love. And that is because they don't know what it means. They have made of it a blend of sensuality, vanity, and hatred,—indeed, you may include in it anything you please. Then it is discovered that there are guilty loves, unwholesome loves; and how the scandal is enjoyed! But there are no varieties of love; there is love or non-love. I don't see any difference between loving a dog, a mother, a friend, or a mistress. Love is the desire to give, not to take. *Kasihan*, say the Malays, or *sayang*. The same word for love and giving, for love and pity . . . *Sayang! Sayang!* Soft lamentation for the beauty, the ugliness of what one loves. The desire to rescue it from life, from suffocation. . . ."

Rolain had never spoken to me in this tone of sombre exaltation. La Roque bent forward to listen, but I did not think he could hear. I, eager and a little embarrassed, heard while affecting not to listen. The things that Rolain had said, these half-expressed confidences of his, seemed beneath the man. Good enough for people who are merely good. This love that gives and does not take,—that was not Rolain, that was common property. Common property, indeed, but only in theory. . . . And then he spoke with such an accent of conviction,—he, usually so aloof and modest. I felt as one must feel when an artist one admires produces a work one does not like, but into which he believes he has put his noblest self. And we find it ignoble! The expression of passion is always a little vulgar. . . . But was I not too sensitive? When Rolain dips ideas in emotion, I feel him nearer to me,—too near, a little below himself. Was, then, my worship for him based on his aloofness? . . . How anti-Christian I must be! And after all what had he said? Next to nothing. But deep down I had felt I knew not what—something, perhaps, of that self that should be kept secret, something too personal,—something like the smell of the man's blood. And it was so unexpected, in the middle of an entertainment! . . . Unexpected? I ought to have understood, of course, that Rolain could only talk in such a fashion at a moment when conversation was almost impossible. Was he, in fact, talking to me, or to himself? I did not hear the last words. That pervasive music had started once again; the shrill voice of the violin above the humming tom-toms. I watched the violinist; he held his instrument on his knees, his bow in his left hand, and swayed his shoulders as he played. There were other instruments,—flageolets, trumpets, I can't remember now. The heat and the music made me dizzy.

But the women got up to dance. They no longer wore boots. Their feet were bare, with rings round their ankles. That was the best point in their costume, and all I can say in its favour. Excess of ornament disfigures. Nothing could be less seductive than such dancing girls. Jerking their forearms, they moved across the stage in stilted poses. Meanwhile the young men of the village still hesitated to face these choreographic stars. The first few were haled on to the platform by the *penghulu's* eldest son. But that encouraged the rest, and soon, with the aid of beer, the performance began to liven up. From time to time the shrill voice of one of the women could be heard uttering a couplet. For want of beauty, they have cultivated their minds, and they know by heart hundreds of epigrams with which they tease the dancers. The Malay public loves these encounters. But at Kampong Nyor the epigrams fell flat. Not one of these boorish villagers could find a word in answer. They went on dancing in heroic silence, with a handkerchief over their mouths as though to withhold a possible rejoinder, and then left the platform in a storm of laughter and hisses.

"Are there only fish here to answer these sea-gulls?" asked Rajah Long in a surly tone.

I looked for Smail among the audience. He got up at once, and his brother with him.

They were a contrast to the young dandies of Kampong Nyor who, in their anxiety to be in the Singapore fashion, had come out in what they conceived to be their choicest attire: white waistcoats, striped blazers from John Small's or Washaway's, tennis shoes soled with crepe rubber, multi-coloured socks and garters, and even open-work women's stockings,—all in addition to their ordinary garb. Beside this naïve display, the Malay costume, at once rich and simple, looked "very neat", as La Roque observed. A short silk sarong round the waist over a suit of sea-green or light yellow silk, loose at the neck, the fore-arms, and the ankles, and on the head the Malayan crimson velvet cap. An easy garment, but so fine and soft that it outlines the muscles of the body like a bathing costume.

The orchestra went on playing the same tune; but the dance was now something that I no longer recognised. The step, too, was the same, but served only to support the movements and poses of the body. The brothers, who came of an old family of Palembang, had kept the true tradition, now lost except in Java or in certain districts of Sumatra. Their movements were undulations that started from an invisible centre, rippled, at the level of the skin, down the arms, the lissom fingers, and beyond them in invisible fluidities; it is the possession of the visible by the invisible, an oriflamme in the wind. Sometimes the movement slackened and broke into little jerks. I thought of slow motion in the cinema, or rather of those children's toys, forerunners of the cinema, in which one can see the gyrations of an acrobat through slits in a revolving cylinder. Then the inner vibration was renewed, and the mechanism came to life once more; pose melted into pose, and the body recovered its suppleness as a snake slips from its crumpled skin.

The women, surprised at first, soon shewed that they knew all about an art whose subtleties they had disdained to display to uncomprehending eyes. They were delighted. Art and kindness can transfigure everything, and they became almost graceful. In courteous stanzas they addressed the dancers as princes of the line of Sang Sapurba, as Argus pheasants, as green beetles; and the brothers countered, using the same rhymes, with compliments to houris and flasks of perfume. The audience applauded vigorously. But Smail having put a trifle of irony into one of his replies, a sharp couplet designated him a duck trying to crow; this he parried with an allusion to a hen that would never lay an egg. After a few skirmishes in this style, the women took offence, stopped dancing and sat down.

Smail was urged to sing. The musicians played several airs in the hope of finding a tune that would inspire him. No one seemed to expect a known song, but an improvisation; that alone has any value. Instead of singing he began to dance; but his purpose was to liberate his body by mechanical activity and seek ideas in the ecstasy of rhythm. Rolain had borrowed La Roque's pocket book. As soon as Smail began to sing, I saw him note down the pantun; then he tore out the page and handed it to me. I kept it, as he never thought to ask for it again. It is the only time I saw his writing and the last. Here is the page. At the top of it were a few scribbled words, a sort of opening recitative announcing the subject:

"Nyor—Kampong Nyor—Kampong Nyor semantan . . ."

Nyor is a coconut, and the place where we were was called the Village of the Coconut.

Nyor semantan is the young nut in which the core is still quite liquid.

A green coconut—you can hear the water in its heart,
A yellowing durian keeps its secrets.

I know why I long for you to be in my hands,
You know not why you wish to meet my lips.

A pantun always speaks of love, but it is only a poetic game. In Smail's improvisation there was something oddly direct, a sharp and urgent tone that struck me. This song of love was addressed to someone in the crowd. Turning towards the group of women I saw Rajah Long's daughter, the girl who had lowered her veil as she passed us on the road, sitting in the first row, with eyes and mouth wide open and her small round face in rapture.

Man is a durian for the pubescent maid,
Hard and bristly—she fears that he will hurt her.

After disgust and fright, comes curiosity,
After curiosity comes ever growing desire.

At the end of each quatrain the orchestra went on alone, drowned by the cries of the audience, the shrill cries of Malays when they are excited, like the cries of women. However, the women, as befitted them, kept silence, motionless under their veils. And yet I thought I could distinguish a sort of agitation in their crouching throng. Rajah Long had turned towards them in an imperious attitude. But I had not time to speculate on the meaning of that gesture. Smail went on:

> Open the fruit of disquieting odour
> And never again can you be sated;
>
> Its seeds, like eggs, slip through the fingers,
> Its cream is strong and sweet like garlic and milk.

The crowd exulted. "Jolly clever!" roared La Roque, crashing his glass down on the table with such vigour that it broke and splashed us with his drink. He seemed scarcely to notice, and shouted for Smail to go on, or start another song. But at a sign from Rajah Long the dancers had got up. Smail left the platform and sat down, with a troubled look on his face. Following the direction of his eyes, I saw a group of women moving off through the crowd, and this time not one of them turned to drop her veil. . . .

"I've had enough," said Rolain suddenly; "Let us go."

In spite of La Roque, who had just at that moment sent for some whisky from the launch —"good stuff, you know, real old Scotch"—we departed. We walked in single file down the path that led by countless windings to the beach. In the dim light and the flat calm the tall *lalang* looked like a solid mass with shining walls. Not a sound could be heard but the tom-tom, a faint booming in the distance. It was like a relief night in the trenches. The body felt strengthless, and the mind empty. . . .

"The little coconut," hummed Ngah behind us,

> The little coconut holds no milk,
> The moon has drunk it.
>
> Nyor semantan bukan
> Nyor di makan bulan.

IV

AMOK

IV

AMOK

I

> Terang bulan terang temaram
> hantu berjalan laki bini

ANOTHER interval, a dead point of existence in which all movement had ceased. The eyes of Fate were turned elsewhere. Such times of stagnation are not unknown in families: not a death for ten or twenty years, and it seems as though nothing will ever change. In the lives of nations Ministries come and go, but all remains the same. Periods of security in which cataclysms ripen to fulfilment. Men live like children who do not realise that they are growing older. There is time to kill time. Eurydice dances with her companions on the grass where the serpent sleeps.

I was back on my plantation. The journey from that distant beach by the China sea took no more than one day: La Roque's new autocar, and my old Ford. I saw nothing of the marvels that had so dazzled me. I wonder what those tourists and writers who speed over the world think they see of it. One or two spots, perhaps, where they lingered a few days, and which they soon ceased to look at. My rapid journey made me understand the vastness of that world which they describe in so summary a fashion.

My own small domain—how vast it was! I walk among the trees I know so well, each of which has its own particular physiognomy, its own little defects. I feel I could almost address them by name. Indeed, at the beginning I used to amuse myself by doing so. The first tree at the corner of the plantation at the entrance happened to be the tallest and the largest. I called him Pater; the second, Noster. I said to myself as I examined them: Sanctificetur needs a whitewash. But they were too many. I had to replace the paternosters, the phrases from the *Aeneid*, by numbers of a series. When I spoke of number 16, row 12, Block VI, the White-Ant Kangany could find it without my help.

The coolies had got a little slack. The impostors and flatterers had already settled into soft jobs. I sent for Joseph; and Joseph appeared. A glorified Joseph, scented, self-satisfied, adorned with tortoise-shell spectacles, with his hands shaved as far as a fringe of glossy hair round his wrists. He expected nothing but praise for his management, but wanted to give me a chance of offering it. "You have been a long time away from your poor plantation, Sir. We thought you were never coming back. We could hardly bear to speak of you. . . ." As I said nothing, he added; "I carried out my duties as well as I could. It was not easy. But a man of my age has a certain authority. The coolies regarded me with deep respect. . . ." This smirking self-gratification annoyed me. I would willingly have recognised his services, but now, I thought, his own praises must be his reward. I only spoke of what there was to criticise. The cleaning of the drains had not been finished. "That," he answered; "was *thanks to* an epidemic of measles that . . ." But the sticky, overcured rubber, the wells full of dead leaves, the herd of dirty goats—your own goats, Joseph,—wandering about the plantation, licking up the latex, upsetting the cups—do you call that measles? I turned my back on him and left him gaping, as futile as his fatuous smile.

Potter, hearing of my return, came to report his inspections of the estate. He hated Joseph, as indeed he hated any deputised authority,—accountant, kangany, and even the higher caste coolies; he had no use for any but pariahs, and the more pariah-like the better. For the first time I stood up to my ex-manager. We argued vehemently about a person for whom we both cared nothing. I knew Joseph was only waiting for an opportunity to complain of Potter's brutality. There was no need; since that conversation he had not a virtue that I would not recognise.

I listened meekly to the other criticisms. Potter did not pick his words. In ten minutes he proved to me that I knew nothing of my job, and that everything at Bukit Sampah was upside down. But he melted when he took his leave. "After all," he said, wagging his head; "it looks something like a rubber estate." Which, coming from that gnarled old mouth, was indeed a eulogy.

I told Potter the great news; we were going to extend our semblance of a rubber estate. Rolain had suggested it on our way back from Pahang. "When no one is planting," he said, "is just the time to plant. Rubber will soon go up with a run. I'm putting all I have into it; and you'll enjoy the job."

Always this taste for risk. Rolain is a born gambler who cares little about the issue. I was appalled by his audacity. But I saw one advantage in the plan: I could keep my coolies. The discharge of coolies, even those whom one would like to murder, is for a planter like a surgical operation self-inflicted—a sort of suicide by flaying. He will try to gain time, invent all manner of pretexts, even resign. Let no one suggest he should reduce his labour force.

It was easy to find contractors to clear the jungle, since there had been no work for them for some time. All the Malays in the country offered their services. I made a careful selection, and got them ridiculously cheap.

The work in the jungle was additional to my usual work on the plantation: I had to choose the ground, delimit it with the help of a prismatic-compass, divide it into sections so that each of the contractors might have his share, and when the felling has begun, stand by to see there was no delay. I had calculated one month for the felling, two months for the debris to dry in the sun, and we should still have time to burn off before the great rains. It would make a glorious conflagration.

The dense undergrowth, through which Malays dart about like monkeys, has first to be chopped away. Then they attack the forest trees. On all sides I hear the axe-blows biting steadily into the trunks. The night moisture falls from the higher branches in great drops. The jungle smells of fresh shavings and crushed leaves. Hour after hour the axes thud against the stems before a single tree falls; the fellers begin by observing the line and angle of the tree, the disposition of the thick encircling network of lianas, and then they cut one deep gash in one side only, so that the tree is left standing. But the colossus that towers above that throng of giants, is the last to be felled, and its collapse will bring down all the rest. Sometimes the structure of it is so vast, it grips the earth with such an array of buttresses, that it has to be surrounded with scaffolding like a cathedral before the cylindrical part of the trunk can be reached. Then, balanced on a frail swaying framework, little brown men nibble at the enormous column. They attack it on both sides. The tapping of the axes on that huge circumference seems almost futile. And yet, little by little, the gashes widen and deepen towards the heart. The tree, by some strange witchery, still holds. I keep on thinking it must fall, I see the head dip slowly, and I shout aloud. . . . The Malays look at me in astonishment. No, it was the movement of the clouds that set everything a-quiver. I must not unnerve these men: they are risking their lives in an attack on an unknown power that may indeed be a tree, or a spirit in the guise of a tree. Is it certain that the sorcerer's incantations, and the white cock he has sacrificed have appeased the dark soul of the jungle? Those men, so easily daunted by any sort of work, seem positively to enjoy the risk, the conflict with the visible and the invisible. Slackening their effort, they listen to the dull vibration that succeeds each blow, mark the tension of the fibres, the rustle of the foliage, and sniff the wind. Soon, very soon, they must leap down, and fly through the brushwood; fly, terrified but victorious, shouting defiance at the thunderous crash.

I often grew tired of watching the exploits of these gnawing insects, and went away. Here was the plantation; fresh air, and wholesome light. And then, suddenly, at my back, I would hear the rending shriek of a tornado; then a moaning sound, a sort of long drawn out neigh that ended in a roar. The earth shook beneath my feet. On a slope of the hill, in a cloud of flying wreckage, a whole stretch of jungle had crashed.

* * * * *

"The Tuan is over-tired," said Ngah when I came back in the evening.

I dropped into a long chair. He knelt down, unrolled my putties with deft finger-tips disentangled my boot laces, and pulled off my mud-caked socks. Between the hills there is always some swamp that must be crossed; and in the centre of the new clearings, there was a torrent from the mountains that dashed into the Sanggor. I often crossed it, choosing the places where a fallen tree might serve as a gangway. It was always a hard job; one had to pick one's way through broken branches and spiny creepers. But I grew more agile, and was proud of my acrobatic prowess. There was, however, one crossing that I did not like. Near the mouth of the torrent, where it flowed between sheer banks, it could only be negotiated by a tree-trunk so steep and slippery that I did not venture on it. I preferred to slide down the clayey slope and take to the water. But it is difficult to swim in all one's clothes and wearing heavy boots. I was often carried away by the current, and had to clamber up the opposite bank by the precarious aid of lianas. I had made that crossing several times, for near by was an old gnarled tree which the Malays refused to cut down. It was a *sialang*, they said, whose sap is poisonous and spurts into your eyes; or else they alleged that hornets had nested in it. I chipped it with a few blows of an axe; the bark and the wood were completely dry, and there was never a sign of a hornet. There must have been some other motive for the respect shewn to this ancient. The contractor whom I questioned would not tell, he merely answered: "He is unwilling to be cut down." And when I pressed him, Matsaman added: "It does not matter, Tuan, the tree is dry, and will burn as it stands."

When I got back I often went to sleep on the veranda. Then Ngah would come and hover round and cough, and if I opened an eye, he said: "Now the Tuan must have a bath. I have laid out the sarong in the bath room." I was so weary that I let myself be undressed and sluiced and soaped. Finally he rubbed me with a solution of alcohol and menthol, which leaves a delicious freshness on the skin, and my weariness was gone.

Then came dinner. Ngah's cookery was rather monotonous, but he made an excellent curry, savagely spiced, the fires of which were extinguished in a *gula malaka*, the Malay dessert, sago diluted with coconut milk, and sweetened with sugar cane caramel.

After that I went back to my long chair and we talked. He had first taught me how to pronounce his name. I used to say N-gah, G-nah, Neeah, which made people smile and embarrassed him on my account. At last I succeeded in pronouncing the *g* and *n* at the same time, as was correct. Half asleep I listened to his stories and fables—among others, his account of the creation of the world.

"*Kun!*" said Allah. "*Kun!*" repeated Muhammad. "Then the sky and the earth were created, the earth as large as a tray, and the sky as a parasol."

"Ah. . . . So they got bigger as they grew older."

"No, Tuan, the soul of the sky and the earth are as large as I say. And the soul of the Tuan is about the size of the top joint of his little finger."

There was no answer to this.

"But surely Muhammad is the Prophet. How could he be born by then?"

"Ah, Tuan," said Ngah impatiently; "it was the soul of Muhammad that said *kun*."

He went on with his story but I listened no longer. I was brooding over the explanation that seemed to him so simple. Souls, then, exist in advance, if one might say so. Or rather, they are not immortal, according to our ideas, but eternal. . . .

One day Ngah expounded the hierarchy of colours. White, the first, is the colour of spirits. Yellow is reserved for Rajahs. Blue is the colour of my Tuan who wears it in his eyes. To himself he allowed the inferior colours that no one else would claim, red and green, one of them to adorn his head, and the other his body.

"And black?" I asked.

"Oh black," he said contemptuously; "black is good enough for Chinamen's trousers. Or for white men—the sort who dance with women."

If I had pointed out that he too had danced with women, he would doubtless have answered that he did not dance with them, but opposite them. However, I would not argue, it was a waste of time. His babble soothed me. I had the sensation of talking to a friendly dog. One need not enquire whether the dog's ideas are very coherent.

On his arrival at Bukit Sampah, Ngah had said at once: "I like this house very much."

He had gone up on to the veranda and surveyed the circle of mountains and the river.

"That is excellent. Water should flow towards a house, and not away from it. All that falling water means money. The Tuan will soon be rich."

One day he brought back a little striped cat that had been given him in the village.

"He eats so little, so very little," he said, as though to excuse himself. "We will give him a small fish's head sometimes."

He explained that a cat was very useful in a house.

"Very useful? You mean he will eat mice?"

This question seemed to puzzle him. . . .

"He may perhaps eat mice as well. . . . But what he wants is to be in a comfortable house where there are many carpets, cushions, and good food. Then he will pray all day for his master's prosperity."

He stroked the little cat who at once began to pray with fervour.

"What is his name?"

"He is called cat, but I shall call him Iskandar."

"Iskandar! That is a grand name!"

"It is the name of a great Malay Rajah who conquered all the earth. . . ."

I looked into the Malay history book, the Sejarah Melayu, which Rolain had lent me, and discovered that Iskandar, ancestor of Sang Sapurba, founder of the Malay dynasty, was Alexander the Great. . . . The East is still full of his legend, and all peoples claim him as their own. Two-horned Iskandar, as the tradition has it. Two-horned, like Moses, like a Hindu deity. . . .

Iskandar was pampered. He did not confine himself to fish's heads, he licked all the plates, and lapped the dregs from the cups. When I had not come by tea-time, I noticed that he had, none the less, been treated to a little of the fragrant orange pekoe that was sent to Potter from his old plantation in Ceylon, and of which he regularly sent me some.

"You will make him ill with that tea. It's too strong for him."

"He asked for it," answered Ngah.

One day I heard screams, as of a slaughtered animal, proceeding from the bath room. There

I found Ngah, with lacerated bleeding arms, engaged in giving Iskandar a bath. I managed to snatch away the little frantic, headless, tailless ball of needles that scratched me too. Ngah told me he had washed the cat to bring on the rain. Fortunately for cats, periods of drought are rare in Malaya.

Ngah had set to work with so much zeal that I had not believed that it could last. He did not bring to his task Ha Hek's mathematical method; but he brought more imagination, an art that surely had its secret rules. From time to time the bungalow was turned upside down; there was a constant din of hammering, I stumbled over ladders, or even found all the furniture in the garden, undergoing a sun cure. Then an armistice followed, and the spiders came back to their lairs. However, my linen was always properly laid out in the wardrobe, on a rigorous system that I was not allowed to modify, my socks and sun helmets were cleaned and ready for me when I needed them, and missing buttons re-appeared. When I undressed, I flung my clothes on to the floor. Ngah picked them up, and, as though by magic, I found clean things waiting for me on a chair, always the same chair, with every object in its appropriate pocket. Occasionally indeed, Ngah would gravely present me with some oddment that had gone about with me for weeks, transferred automatically from one pocket to another, something that had lost significance and became a parasite,—a bit of string or an old piece of bark; "Does the Tuan really still need this?"

But one of the principal advantages of Ngah's service was that no accounts were ever kept. Oh those reckonings with Ha Hek! How I loathed to see him approaching with his little note book when I was just about to take a rest. I at once realised that I was far too busy to be able to waste time in that way. . . . Now, I had only to hand out money when I was asked for it. Indeed Ngah had merely to help himself from a supply that was always lying loose on a corner of the table. In the East, a man is never so thoroughly robbed, nor in more humiliating a fashion, as when he has taken precautions to protect himself. Prudence is the mother of catastrophe. I did not forget that Ha Hek had searched my drawers without the aid of keys.

Blessed era of tranquillity! I now had a house steward who never asked me what he had to do. I could thus reserve all my power of initiative for the plantation, and rule my subjects with a will intact.

No cares are so irksome as those of domesticity; and for the most part I was spared them. I say—for the most part; because I had in my service a Tamil water carrier. A tall, upstanding fellow, a magnificent type of pariah. He always looked as though he were accomplishing some solemn rite, even when he removed the night soil. Ngah ordered this personage about in very peremptory fashion. Sometimes I heard cries: "Aya! Aya! Ayoyo!" I hurried up. "He has been beating me," moaned Govindasamy. Tears were trickling down his vast black chest. Beside him stood the diminutive figure of Ngah, with an impassive, obstinate expression on his face that seemed to say; "You may perhaps disapprove of me, but I have done my duty."

He assumed the same sullen look when I had received a visit from Palaniai. On these occasions he served me with cold correctness, waited until he was called, and answered in monosyllables. It made me quite uncomfortable, and I really felt as though I had done wrong. At table, when I unfolded my napkin, no flower dropped from it.

Sometimes I did not even know what had made him so sulky; and I asked him to explain. What had I said, or what had I done to wound his feelings? He remained impenetrable. "I shall beat you," I said. "Beat me if you will," he replied, and threw me an evil glance.

Then suddenly, without apparent reason, I noticed that the cloud had dissolved. Ngah came once more and crouched at my feet in the evening, humming pantuns, and trying to evade an explanation. But I am of a race that wants to understand, and is not conspicuous for tact.

"Tell me," I said; "have you any complaint? Do I abuse you? or beat you? You know my *liver* is not evil. . . ."

In the face of so much insistence, he had to answer, but he did so with a wry and hesitant look:

"The Tuan's liver is like his chin; it is smooth one way, and rough the other. . . ."

* * * * *

As I was one day looking for a book, I came by chance on an old gardening catalogue; and it occurred to me that my garden was neglected.

In some of his idle moments Govindasamy did a little digging here and there. Unmethodical toil that led to no visible result. I wanted a profusion of flowers, great masses of brilliant colour that would stand out against the dark background of the jungle and the cold blue of the mountains: red flowers, yellow flowers, blossoms of the heat, irradiating light like the door of a furnace. Hibiscus, with its tongues of flame, I already had. But canna, alamanda, amaranth . . . Yes, a great bed of carmine amaranth, with long sinuous leaves, like gushing fountains under the glare of a search-light. Ngah received the charge of resuscitating the garden, with Govindasamy as staff; and counsels of moderation.

Night and morning, from the vantage of my veranda, I surveyed all the phases of the struggle against the stubborn weeds, and the re-establishment of order. The road up to the bungalow soon described a fine regular curve between freshly shorn stretches of green sward; flower-beds were laid out, and there was nothing now to do but to order the seeds. I should be able to get them at Kuala Paya, but to aid my choice I plunged into my catalogue. It was fragrant and agreeable reading after a heavy day's work. I never grew weary of the ravishing descriptions that made even the dullest shades of colour sound delightful: "Frosted satin pink"; "A delicate shade of pale dawn pink"; I felt I might purchase the seeds of all the plants on earth.

Shrubs I must have too, and fruit trees. I ordered some grafted mango plants from Calcutta, and I got cuttings of tulip tree, poinsettia, and young traveller's palms from Potter. Every evening, in the refuge of my mosquito net, I read and re-read the catalogues, marking my fancies with a cross, and I fell asleep murmuring their Latin names, and those magic adjectives that so stirred my dreams: *spectabilis*, *cristata*, *suaveolens vel coelestis*, *amplifrons*, *odoratissimus*, *hystrix*. . . .

II

At Kuala Paya, the first Saturday of the month is Planters' Day. They appear early in the morning, by every train and every road, to fetch the pay money from the bank. The town awakes in agitation like a nest of white ants invaded by red ants. There is a new element in the air,—gay, brutal, reckless. Voices are more resonant, and rickshaws go faster. This access of fever lasts until midday. At noon the gun-shot from the fort on the hill releases a centripetal movement that carries everyone to the club.

The planters, who are fond of nicknames, had called this club "The Spotted Dog"; for the reason that, unlike other clubs, which insist on an unimpeachable white skin, this one admitted members more or less tinged with a darker hue, Eurasians, and even pure Tamils. They seldom came, but they had the proud pleasure of paying their subscriptions.

The hair-dressing saloon was kept by a magnificent Hindu, assisted by several apprentices. On leaving the bank I often came in there to enjoy a little doze, while aerial scissors clicked hypnotically round my head, and deft fingers performed a massage of my skull, that looked like a conjuring trick. Under the gentle treatment I felt as if all my troubles were dispelled, my clarity of mind restored.

Soothed and perfumed from the hands of this magician, I made my way towards the bar. It was packed. The semi-circular counter, edged by an unbroken line of lifted elbows, was inaccessible. But beyond it were a few little cane tables and chairs for those whose thirst was not so urgent. The company always arranged itself in geographical order, and I was familiar with the zone of occupation assigned to my district. But I had not taken three steps in that direction before I was observed, caught by many hands, forced into a chair with a large gin-sling in front of me that had been waiting for me since midday, and all glasses were lifted in my honour. I could not understand this ovation, and was quite bewildered by the tumult.

"Silence! Silence!" thundered Bedrock.

All were silent.

"Gentlemen, it is my duty, and it is my pleasure, to present to you today the last specimen of an extinct race: the planter who plants. Yes, gentlemen, it does exist; it is a being who breathes as we do, who drinks gin-slings,—and also plants. In these times of deep depression, while in the seclusion of their City offices our financiers are cowering over their balance-sheets, tearing out their last white hairs. . . ."

"Hear, hear!" growled Potter.

". . . . white hairs . . . Well, blast the financiers! Here is the champion of rubber, the subduer of the jungle, and he belongs to our District. Gentlemen, I give you the pioneer District—Sungei Sanggor!"

Tremendous applause. The bar, and the adjoining territories, surged towards this triumphant district.

"Three cheers for the Planting Planter!"

Three cheers were given, followed by the cry of the Malayan tiger: "Rrrraumph!" Then, all in a circle, with joined hands and marking time with their elbows, they sang; "For he's a jolly good fellow" to the tune that we have borrowed for "Malbrough s'en va-t-en guerre". More hurrahs and tiger-roars. Flowerpet, unbuckling his leather belt, tried to make it into a crown for me, with the great key rings dangling over my ears. Old Holmwood had hoisted himself on to a table, and there stood, with congested eyes and violet cheeks, trampling on broken glasses and brandishing a cane chair:

Voici le sâbre, le sâbre, le sâbre,
Voici le sâbre, le sâââbre de monn père! . . .

When I was able to slip away from this infernal ovation, I observed, among a group of townsmen who had been viewing the scene with indulgent smiles, a man who was making signs to me. I knew him by sight; it was Freeborn, the lawyer. A mane of red hair, bright eyes, and a bull-dog jaw.

"Are you not Monsieur . . . ? Yes . . . I was just about to write to you. I wonder if you would mind looking in at my office today. Three o'clock—will that do? Good,—see you later, then."

* * * * *

"One moment," said the Chinese clerk, getting up from a table covered with files; "I will ask if Mr. Freeborn is willing to see you."

He tip-toed slowly up the stairs, and stopped, with a propitiatory smile composed of thirty-two gold teeth, as soon as his head was at the level of the first floor landing. Five minutes passed. I sat on the table.

"What?" suddenly burst forth a powerful voice that made the clerk jump. "Yes, bring him up."

Freeborn, without looking at me, pointed a finger at a chair. He was turning over a file, grunting and pursing his lips as he fingered the pages; when he got up to put it away I thought he was going to devour it. He took down another, opened it, and placed it before me.

"There; just sign your name."

"Sign my name? What do you mean?"

He fell back in his chair with a groan that was more like a bellow.

"You mean you won't sign? Good God! I don't understand you people. Never satisfied. Always suspicious. What's the objection? Do you want me to read it to you?"

I had lost the use of words.

"Look here," he went on in a weary tone, but a little mollified; "It's all perfectly in order. Here is the title deed; here is the price. That's what you paid, isn't it?"

"But I haven't bought anything . . ."

"Damnation! Have I got to waste my time over such . . . such . . . . Soo Seng, send up two glasses of water."

He swallowed his at a gulp.

"That's to set you an example. Personally I don't like water, and I don't need it. But at your age, all those cocktails . . ."

I felt perfectly clear in the head, but his gaze magnetised me, and to please him I drank my glass of water.

"Feeling better? Well, my friend, not only have you bought this property, but you have paid for it. The vendor, M. Rolain, has given notice of the sale and even deposited the costs of transfer, which is unusual; but it's all the same to me. Bukit Sampah Estate, a hundred thousand dollars. A good bit of business. If you didn't look so flabbergasted, I should say you were a good hand at a bargain. . . . There, just sign that, and you can go away with your blasted plantation under your arm. Pray sign."

That prayer sounded so much like a threat that I signed without knowing very well what I was doing.

He sighed:

"God bless us all. The smallest piece of business is always full of unexpected difficulties. . . . The soul of man is very complex."

He walked with me to the staircase.

"Men are absurd, and nearly all of them mad. The least mad are those who are called dreamers. Yes. The greatest man of all time was a Frenchman like you. You ought to be proud of him. Do you know whom I mean?"

He stared at me with a piercing look, and I was so bewildered by the scene that I nearly said Napoleon, whom I do not like. Freeborn would have killed me. But he was in no doubt of what I was going to reply.

"Jaurès," he murmured. "Yes . . . Jaurès. . . ."

* * * * *

A dense rain was falling as I drove back. I could scarcely see the road and I skidded round the bends, driving fast, and thinking of what I was going to say to Rolain. What was this new folly? I could not understand it. Was he proposing to leave me? . . . He was certainly just the man to go off without a word. But people should not do such things. He might at least have warned me. I was made to look like a fool . . . However, whether the place stood in his name or in mine, all the profits should go to him. Besides, there was nothing to prevent me transferring the plantation back to him. . . . Squalls of rain swept under the hood and lashed my face, cold rivulets coursed down my neck, and I was sitting in a pool of water. Little by little, I felt my ideas grow as indistinct as the contours of the landscape. The hum of the motor, the louder hiss of the rain on the metal surfaces, throbbed in my head.

But when I arrived at Bukit Sampah, a pallid Ngah almost flung himself under my wheels.

"I came back to wait for the Tuan, but we must go at once to the Tuan Rolain's, Smail is very ill. Perhaps he is dead by now. . . ."

On the steep path up to Rolain's house I tried to get some further details. It was not, Ngah said, an ordinary illness. Yes, there was fever too, but it was a kind of madness. Smail recognised no one, and he yelled incessantly; and with a voice that was not his own. Perhaps a . . . a . . . But I could see very well that Ngah did not dare to utter the word "devil" in the jungle.

We reached the clearing. The rain had stopped. Through the gap in the jungle, a large low sun fixed us with a red eye from beneath a mass of dark clouds. Ngah shielded his eyes with both his hands. He always avoided looking at the setting sun and could not understand the pleasure it gave me, an unwholesome pleasure, he thought, and one savouring of bravado. Today I could better understand his uneasiness. The dim world was veiled in heavy wreathing vapours, the exhausted jungle was silent, and the sun, still alive though near to death,—the sun fell as an enemy falls, with a look of hatred.

My clothes were so wet that I stopped before going into Rolain's house to take them off and wring them out; and I made haste, for the silence of the house oppressed me. I was at the foot of the staircase, shivering with cold, and unnerved by fatigue, the surprises of the day, alcohol, anxiety . . . Suddenly, as I raised my eyes towards the veranda, I stood fascinated; right in front of me were two glaring but unseeing eyes, extraordinary eyes, empty, grey, almost white, like the ghostly eyes of statues. . . .

Ngah's voice shook me from my stupor. "It is Pa Daoud, the *pawang*, a great sorcerer. . . ."

The great sorcerer was most singularly ugly. Bare, skinny limbs like leathery parchment, a long yellow shrivelled face, a prominent upper lip, with the tense aspect of an abscess. And all around him, scattered on the floor, an array of boxes, pots, and little heaps of powder.

Suddenly the huddled corpse grew animated, seized two handfuls of grey powder, stood straight up facing towards the West, and flung them at the sun. Three times he bent and rose, battling frantically to dispel that malignant receding disc. And each time his hoarse voice hurled anathemas.

> Mambang kuning mambang kelabu
> Pantat kuning di sembor abu

> Yellow ghost, grey ghost,
> May your yellow hind-quarters be lashed with cinders!

cried the old man, which seemed to me a very rash irreverence; Ngah, in terror, prostrate on a corner of the stair, had covered his head with his sarong so that he could neither see nor hear. Then, suddenly, another cry rose up, a cry that pierced my very marrow, but was like nothing I had ever heard; so deep and yet so shrill, so prolonged, that it might well have been the answer of the ghost. I flung down my clothes, and leapt into the house, slamming the doors behind me. On the floor of one of the rooms was Rolain trying to master Smail. . . . But was it Smail? A devil, a knot of serpents, a contorted being, that bent and stiffened, and then leapt forward in convulsive jerks, like a dying beast whose limbs still gallop in the void.

For hours we wrestled. The four of us could hardly hold him down. What amazing reserves of force were contained in that frail young body! As we held him rigid against the floor, we could see his muscles twist and his nerves vibrate at the level of the skin. When the shrieking ceased we could hear his teeth grind dreadfully against each other. His eyeballs had slipped upwards and only reappeared to look at us in the horror of incomprehension. Whom did he think us? I saw the rage and terror in his face succeeded by the despairing expression of a tortured man who expects nothing from his torturers but death, and nothing from death but the aggravation of his agony, as if about to enter, flayed alive, the fires of hell. But expression is scarcely the word for that ravaged glare, haunted by visions, or lost in the limbo of the unimaginable.

From time to time the crisis was suddenly broken, the contractions ceased, though the muscles were not relaxed, and what lay beneath our hands was a hardened rigid body, limbs of wood. "His soul has gone," said Pa Daoud. We could hear the familiar sound of the wind, the drip of the branches, the cry of a night bird. And we recovered our sense of reality. Here we were at the House of Palms. This was Smail. He had a cataleptic fit. I wiped my sweat-soaked arms.

But Pa Daoud, who was on the alert, made a sign to us.

"Listen! His brother is calling. . . ."

From the outer darkness came a sharp bark, repeated at regular intervals and gradually drawing nearer. I had learned to understand the language of the jungle. I knew it for the high clear call of the hunting tiger. And as though he were indeed answering a call, Smail suddenly wrenched himself free and leapt to the window. The wooden bars cracked, the mosquito gauze gave way, and as we held his legs he turned to bite.

At last, about midnight, the tiger, who seemed to have been ranging round the house, departed. Smail grew calmer. Ngah was able to make us some tea. The moment was favourable, said Pa Daoud, for exorcising the sick man. While he was making his preparations I asked Rolain what had happened.

Smail, Rolain explained, had seemed uneasy for several days past. He gave up reading, no longer dared to go out into the jungle, and slept as soon as his work was done. He had noticed on the trunk of a tree that was visible from that very window one of those phosphorescent lichens that the Malays believe are inhabited by the souls of nocturnal beasts not yet born. The little gleam seemed to fascinate him every night. He clearly saw disturbing omens everywhere; that was quite obvious although he said nothing about it. One day he flung down a book as though the touch of it had burnt him. The binding was covered with little viscous drops, exudations of wood that sometimes fall from the beams in the roof. For him they were the seed of demons. . . .

On the previous night a tiger had been prowling round the house. The glitter of its eyes had been seen. Rolain took down his gun, but Smail had said: "No, Tuan, I beg you not to kill it; who knows what it may be?" When Pa Daoud had said: "His brother is calling," he may have been thinking likewise. There had been an elder brother in the family who died of that mysterious ailment called convulsions. These occur when the soul is struggling forth to possess another body, and when the subject does not die, it is sometimes because the exchange of souls is accomplished; but he is no longer what he was, he is the same only in aspect. The elder brother had died. He had been crossed in love—dismissed by a girl's parents. So that his liver had no more desire to live and his soul had departed. . . .

Pa Daoud's abscess had risen into his cheek. I then realised that his upper lip served him as a tobacco pouch. He finally extracted the quid with his forefinger and threw it into a corner of the room.

He had prepared his *mise en scène ;* a few jars covered with yam leaves, a large bunch of flowers adorned with artificial birds of plaited palm, and, on a brass tray, a pot of incense and bowls of rice. He waved away the lamp. The spirits detest its smell of kerosene and its too emphatic light. Three little tapers flickered in the darkness.

A pinch of incense on the hot embers which Ngah has just brought in. The smoke mounts in a thin vertical column, and Pa Daoud contemplates it, motionless, awaiting the first omen. In a moment or two it bends gently towards him in a faint compliance. Then, with both his hands the wizard breaks the shaft of smoke, gathers it into the palms of his hands and slowly inhales it. The smoke seems to intoxicate him. He sways slightly and his triple shadow flickers on the wall.

The incense had bowed towards him; that means than an invisible being accepts his offering and consents to help him.

"Peace on thee, Tanju!" chants Pa Daoud.

I know thy name and whence thou camest
Thou art impure but sanctified
Born of the mucus from Muhammad's eyes
When he fled from Mekkah
In the dust of the desert
Guided by an infidel
Closing his eyes that were blind from weeping . . .

Nothing impresses the spirits so much as to hear themselves reminded of their origin. It deprives them of the mysterious prestige which they fancy they enjoy among human beings.

And when he who addresses them adds to this proof of mastery allusions to the sacred texts that betray a true servant of Allah, they are completely in subjection.

Pa Daoud knows how to profit by this feeling without abusing it. He picks up the bunch of flowers, holds it out to the smoke, which he then blows downwards on to the blossoms.

> Come into thy garden of delight
> Full of perfumes and of birds
> Created by Allah
> Offered by my brother Smail
> Accept this garden of delights
> Show me the sickness of my brother Smail

All that is asked of this spirit is a diagnosis; and he will indicate it by the disposition of some grains of roasted rice sprinkled over some water in a jar. The grains float, and the sorcerer bends over them; for a long while he watches them in silence.

"I see that it is invisible," murmurs Daoud at last.

And turning towards us, he adds:

"It is a *badi.*"

Then he departed. We heard him walk down the steps of the veranda, enter the jungle and move off into the distance. He is not afraid of the tiger. . . . For my part I was glad to take my bath in the kitchen that evening.

Rolain said that Pa Daoud would come back, that what we had seen were merely preliminaries. The real business would be the encounter with the *badi*.

A *badi* is not a demon, it is something more impersonal, a malignant entity that inhabits all living things, animals, plants, stones, and smoke. . . . It might almost be described as a fluid essence, a power of obsession. Thus, it is the *badi* that passes from the eyes of the tiger and the snake into the eyes of their victims, that glares malignantly from the face of a passer-by, and casts a shadow over the daylight; it is the *badi* that gleams in the rays of the setting sun, in the heavy hour of fear. But an attempt to define it destroys the intuition of what it is. Suffice it to say that there are degrees in the immaterial domain, and that if the demons are evil beings, the *badi* is merely a potentiality, like the germ of an evil deed.

"I explain this very badly," Rolain admitted. "The mind of man is too clear for these subtleties; it is like a sheet of glass through which the light passes, by which it is not decomposed."

Pa Daoud soon re-appeared. He brought with him seven small branches from seven different trees that he had gathered in the jungle. Rolain recognised some of them as being credited with occult properties. I wondered how, in that impenetrable darkness, Pa Daoud had been able to find what he sought. But was he not alleged to see in the dark like a tiger, and even to have the power of turning into a tiger? He often disappeared for days and weeks together. . . .

He took his place once more beside Smail and sat, huddled and motionless, with the palms of his hands on his knees, isolated in a long effort of concentration. Then, little by little, the accumulated force seemed to overflow, sweeping through the limbs like an electric current, shaking the man's whole body. The machine was ready for the conflict.

Flowers are not offered to the *badi*. The garden of delights is put aside. Beauty is not for evil creatures who do not deserve nor appreciate it; indeed, they do not notice it. There it is for all to see, but it must be desired. Those for whom the world is dark see it so because they are looking into the darkness of their own souls. There is no paradise and no hell, but only, in the eyes of men, a vision that makes paradise or hell of what they see.

Pa Daoud's body now sways with a movement recalling the dance of the cobra beset by enemies, alert, elastic, with menace and fear in its cold eyes. Then the lips begin to move. Magic formulae, to be more effective, must come from far away, they must find inspiration in the deep places of the mind, just as the breath that shoots the arrow from a blow pipe must come from deep down in the lungs. The words hover, as yet unuttered, on the magician's quivering lips. Then comes the voice, hoarse at first, but soon incisive as an arrow. But not one of us can understand the meaning of those hissing sounds. Rolain told me in a whisper that it was the language of the spirits. Against his impalpable adversary the sorcerer calls to his aid occult allies in a sphere where inarticulate words are understood. Thus, when thunder growls, the dog's troubled eyes seek comfort in the eyes of man.

The strange sounds grow insensibly more distinct, until they could, it seems, be written down in the letters of our alphabet. Among them are Arabic words, and I recognised some names. Pa Daoud was invoking the four Archangels: Israfil, master of the elements, Azrail, master of animate beings, Mikail, who feeds and fertilises, Jibrail, who instructs. He returns once more to Israfil, the furthest and most transcendant, the ultimate Archangel who can still hear the prayers of men; beyond is silence, and the will of Allah.

Emboldened by these Great Ones, the sorcerer stands up and calls upon the *badi* in harsh tones. He speaks in Malay, and it matters little whether the *badi* understands or even hears; the appeal is made articulate, and the sacred frenzy will act through the aid of the protecting powers.

> O *Badi!* O *Badi!* O *Badi!*
> Enter into this bunch of leaves
> Absorb the sap of these leaves

The seven antidotes of these leaves
Return to the places from which thou camest
In the water that flows and trickles
In the wind that passes and does not return
In the red abysses of the earth
To the herbless plains
To the shoreless seas
To the stretchless spaces
By the virtue of La-ilaha-illa-llah . . .

In a hand that no more trembles he holds out the bunch of leaves to the purifying incense, and then sweeps it seven times over Smail's stiffened body from the head to the feet. The *badi* must go forth and the frightened soul must now return. The body must not remain untenanted, or it would fall into decay. Pa Daoud summons the soul with the word the Malays use to call their chickens: *Kur! Kur!*

"*Kur! Semangat!* Come, soul of Smail bin Bangka! Come, ye seven souls! . . . Come, bird, come, little one, come, shadowy one. . . ." And indeed, at that very moment, the body quivers under the tickling twigs, and suddenly the soul returns. The soul? I should say seven shrieking souls . . . We sprang up, ready to help. But the sorcerer swept us aside with an arm that cut like a lash, and, bending over Smail, gripped him by the head, glared into his eyes and screamed; screamed louder even than the sick man, without taking breath. There they crouched like two dogs baying at death. And then they both fell back exhausted.

I remember that night as a vigil for the dead, fading now and then into unconsciousness, and I emerged from one of those heavy torpors only to fall into an hallucination. Around me lay abandoned bodies—corpses, perhaps. I no longer recognised the faces. There they lay, in a misty darkness pierced by three quivering yellow flames that distorted their features into a grin, nondescript but terrible, like the face of a dead German I had seen years before, in the loop-hole of a trench, turn green and gradually dissolve.

In a circle of light lay a long dessicated mummy. Dead, utterly dead, six thousand years before. Yes, I remembered, he had been a sorcerer, and had defied the sun. He had blasphemed Hammon-Ra, the hawk-headed god . . . Crouching like a sphinx, then bursting into a frenzy. He talked the language of the spirits . . . To the stretchless spaces—what did that mean? . . . Everything grew dim. I was lost in a murk of confusion.

The void: then something moving in the far depths, a needle slipping into the consciousness, a feeling of uneasiness, a quiver of the eyelids,—corpses once again. Beside the mummy, a corpse. And at my side the outline of someone who may be alive or dead, or may never have existed; and as I look at him he recedes and fades away. I feel I must pursue this unknown creature, bring him back, and hold and understand him, if that were possible. But I have no strength and the darkness again comes upon me. Eternal darkness.

A faint stir in the silence—like the sound of wind. Something that at last recalls to reality. The wind of morning. The candles had gone out. Morning would suddenly be here; all would be clear to our eyes and minds. The window was already a strictly rectangular rectangle. I heard and recognised the rasping call of the jungle cocks. The spell was loosed. How good it was to wake!

"Let him sleep," said Rolain in a low voice; I guessed he was speaking of me, and I opened my eyes.

It was full daylight. Smail still lay outstretched, but his face was calm. He had been undressed so that his sweat-soaked garments might be changed. The fever had nearly gone. Pa Daoud was bending over him, and with a circular motion of his flat hand was rubbing his chest with a sort of polished shining ball, about the size of an orange, brown in colour with a strange green iridescence; and Rolain said; "That is a bezoar."

"Bezoar?" I searched my memory. Bezoar of Ispahan, bezoar of Golconda. . . . I thought it was a precious stone.

I waited until Pa Daoud had finished rubbing the body and I asked him.

"It is the most precious of all stones," he answered; "even more precious than gold. Gold of course has its uses. But what is the use of rubies, opals, moonstones, and the rest?"

I took it in my hand. It was quite light, and could have nothing in common with a stone. Rolain said it was a deposit that formed in the stomach of certain animals.

"This is a porcupine bezoar," said Pa Daoud confidentially; "the rarest of all. I have one from a red monkey, but they are smaller. This one was given me by the Sakais in the high mountains near the source of the Balungar. They are very ignorant, almost like monkeys."

"Is it far from here?"

"At least twenty chews of tobacco, but if the paths are blocked it is much farther. I had cured their chief. They had this and did not know how to use it. They just kept it. The stone is a very old one; but it is still growing."

"Growing?"

"It was almost dead,—dried up. I fed it in a box, on rice. I gave it nothing to drink and it is thirsty, and when I rub it on human bodies it drinks up all evil humours, running sores, and the acid of the liver. . . ."

Smail was listening. He had recognised his old master, from whom he learned religion and poetry, but he was so weak that he could not talk and only his eyes seemed alive.

"He'll get well, won't he?"

"How do I know? The *badi* is powerful . . . ."

"But," said Rolain, in a firm voice, looking at Smail, "Allah is more powerful."

Pa Daoud bowed.

"Yes, when there is nothing else, there is Islam—acceptation."

We remained silent for a moment.

"However I'll give him some quinine, all the same," said Rolain.

III

Ngah now went up every day to the House of Palms, and as the news he brought back was reassuring, I used to stay at home of an evening, tired after my day's work. Pa Daoud, said Ngah, often came to see Smail, he did a little cooking and talked a great deal to Tuan Rolain. But Smail did not speak. He merely listened and reflected.

Every time that I made ready to go, some unforeseen occurrence held me back; a breakdown in the factory engine, a brawl among the coolies, or a palaver. Or some strange animal was brought in for my collection, a sloth, a cameleon, a flying lemur. When I asked what these animals fed on, I was told that they ate rice, with a smile at my naïvety. And in fact Ngah distributed great bowls of rice in my menagerie, which did not, however, prevent the mortality there being very high. He once suggested sewing up the eyelids of an argus pheasant to tame it, telling me that in a few days the bird would be no longer afraid of me and its sight could be restored; but it seemed to me less cruel to expose it to my awful appearance. I was wrong. It had to be released. I merely kept two handsome feathers as penholders for my office.

I had to devote all my time to the estate. The white ants were giving trouble. Poisoned sugar, an emulsion of petrol and soapy water, fumigations with carbon sulphide,—nothing was of any avail. Here and there, trees that looked perfectly healthy and gave abundant latex, suddenly collapsed in a breath of wind; their roots had been eaten away. I had the ground dug up all round them; hundreds of little red ants forthwith descended on their enemies, seized the termites by their white bellies and scuttled away with them; even the warriors were thus ignominiously removed, with their heads in the air and foolishly snapping their formidable jaws. I relished this massacre; I should have liked to see the responsible kangany devoured in just the same way, but he was my best kangany, so I had to be satisfied with heartily abusing him in Tamil fashion,—himself, his father and his mother, and all the generations that had gone before him. A paltry revenge. A few termites the less, a black face that turned to grey,—but I knew that all around me millions of my little enemies were tirelessly pursuing their unseen labours. The queens, in the security of their subterranean lairs, were busy laying eggs and manufacturing their own subjects faster than we could destroy them. I realised that there was only one remedy, and that was to capture the queens. I put twice as many coolies on to the work. Deep saps were dug, and the conflict carried on by trench fighting, and by bribery. Every evening the prisoners were mustered. I paid ten cents apiece for the precious queens, and twenty cents when they were as large as my thumb; and then I gave them back to the sellers, who at once devoured these fat juicy sweets with relish.

I don't know why I tell these stories about the ants. If I were writing a novel they would come better at the beginning. But I want to fix these last memories of my life as a planter, no doubt because they were the last. I remember, too, that about this time I spent long hours in the factory. Until then I had rather neglected the technical side of the industry. I looked on it as mechanical, unworthy of a man of action, hardly more attractive than accounts. Suddenly it began to interest me. I loved to watch the latex poured from brimming buckets into the troughs, the foam skimmed off with broad wooden palettes, the surface of the liquid gradually grow resistant, elastic under the pressure of the fingers, delicate as flesh. The curdled mass was then laid out on long tables, where it was cut up; and it emerged from the rollers in broad strips of rough linen.

The factory smelt acridly of whey, and hummed with the rhythmic whirr of the motor and machinery, and the hiss of rushing water. At the far end of the factory Joseph superintended the weighing and packing of the crepe, which, once dry, took on an amber transparency. Hammers rattled on the packing cases. Through the great open doors I could see the areca tree avenue, like a double colonnade of slender shafts topped by bouquets of palms, and the passing carts drawn by great white Indian bullocks. Dimly, and against my own consent, all this seemed a little more my own and held my interest more closely than before. I was annoyed to find myself feeling so, and I realised that I must speak to Rolain,—I would not have him believe that I had taken his gift without a word of acknowledgement. But I fancy the instinct of property had slyly slipped into my mind, and I let the days pass. . . .

* * * * *

The white ant gang were hard at work digging. In that deep pit, and on those heaps of red earth, the sweating bodies of the Tamils gleamed in the sun with a blue metallic lustre. From time to time, one of them stopped, loosened his hair, flung it sharply backwards, and then, with elbows in the air, knotted it against his neck. All their gestures were harmonious and pleasing. They did not spit on their hands as workmen do in Europe. They worked with vigour but also with composure. Work, among these men who are almost slaves, looks more like a game than a curse.

We had just reached the termites' nest, a great grey sack embedded in the fresh soil, when I saw Joseph approaching. Joseph on the plantation! And running too! So out of breath that he could not speak. I expected news of a catastrophe. He at last gasped out that the Controller of Labour had come to visit the estate and wanted to see me.

"Certainly," I said; "I will come at once." Have the horn blown and let everyone assemble by the coolie lines. There is no need for all this excitement. Why didn't you send a coolie to find me?"

"I wanted to speak to you, sir. Don't you think I could send Gopal III to the village? I'll find some pretext—I'll say he's gone to buy provisions. . . ."

Gopal III? Ah yes. The day before, Gopal III had made a little scene in the factory, and I had been annoyed. He had stood aside while the other tappers were pouring their latex into the vats, and complained to the assemblage that he had been struck by Joseph. A blow from Joseph could not have been a very painful matter. However, he declared he would not stay on an estate where coolies were struck.

Suddenly he looked round wide-eyed, for he saw me close at his side, quite unexpectedly. Standing as he was on a block of cement, he was just at a convenient height; and he got a couple of boxes on the ear that cracked like pistol shots. He fell from his pedestal.

Silence. Consternation. Within Tamil memory no such thing had ever been seen on this estate where coolies were struck. A stick, well and good—that was in the tradition; but a box on the ear! . . .

When I turned to Joseph the crowd fell back respectfully; and Joseph, to whom I said; "I think that came just at the right moment," observed: "Sir, you are the instrument of the Almighty."

But now that the Controller of Labour, W. G. Wootton, Esq., had appeared on the scene, the instrument of the Almighty was no more than a breaker of the law. Joseph stared at me with great startled eyes.

"You are a fool, my dear Joseph," I said; "What I did yesterday I would do as well before a horde of Controllers and the King of England himself. Gopal will stay with the rest. Get along."

All the working coolies were drawn up on the muster ground. The Controller first examined the children,—the boys with nothing but a string round the waist, the girls with a silver heart placed where the fig leaf ought to be,—felt their little fat bellies, poked his thumb into their spleens, and pulled down the skin of their cheeks to look at the inside of their eyelids.

Then it was the women's turn. Most of them complained of imaginary ills, or of each other. "I know all about that," said Wootton; "now let's see the men." He walked down the line, putting a few questions here and there. Suddenly I saw Joseph give a start. The Controller had stopped by Gopal III and was questioning him. I moved away, not wishing to intimidate the victim. But Gopal's clear voice soon broke the silence:

"It is a very good plantation," he said. "The master is our father and our mother, and what he does is right. He knows us, he does not need the help of those who do not know us."

"All right, old chap," growled Wootton, and he turned to me; "That's an awkward sort of fellow, you'd better keep your eye on him."

Then followed a brief inspection of the lines. To draw my attention to some garbage Wootton pushed it aside with his foot as he walked. Then a visit to the latrines which no one had ever used, and he observed: "They are the only buildings in a plantation that are clean and don't smell. Most inviting they look, and it would be a pleasure to be the first visitor. Anyhow, don't be down-hearted. The essential thing is to have latrines. It's the law, and maybe some maniac will try them for fun and set an example that the whole blessed crowd will follow." After which the wells were inspected, and the hospital. We were followed by a single file of kanganies who belched energetically to bear witness to the excellent and abundant food supplied on the plantation. Wootton was unimpressed. He said he was often greeted by that concert, and it was certainly less melodious than silence; but silence was an alarming symptom. It was quite clear that my coolies were happy and well treated. On our way back we passed the school, whence came a convincing babble of shrill voices.

"Excellent," said Wootton. "Excuse me for having come without letting you know. I didn't have time. Devilish hot, isn't it? I suppose you've got some ice at your place?"

The ferryman was waiting for us on the river bank with his punt. As we got out on the other side by the bungalow, in a narrow creek that I used to call Bukit Sampah harbour, I suddenly noticed Smail. He was just untying the painter of my little canoe. As he saw me, he hesitated for a second, then, still holding the cord in one hand, he saluted me with the other.

"*Tabeh*, Tuan. My Tuan has allowed me to go home. . . . I did not know where to find my Tuan. Would the Tuan kindly lend me. . . ."

I did not like anyone using that fragile dug-out which I kept for myself to practice canoeing. Besides, it was very easy to upset, and an unwary coolie had nearly drowned himself in it not long before. Nothing of the kind was to be feared with Smail. But yet I hesitated.

I had no time to reflect. Wootton was getting impatient, and thinking only of the whisky and soda that was waiting for us at the bungalow. Smail took my silence for acquiescence, crouched bare-shouldered in the stern of the canoe and thrust it into the current.

We had stayed late on the plantation and yonder in the jungle the sun was sinking. It was the hour when all colours are intensified. I watched the canoe speed away, leaving slanting golden ripples in the sluggish water. Suddenly I thought of Rolain. A vague impression had just crossed my mind, the memory of something he had said to me. . . . Ah, yes. . . . That Kris . . . The slender craft dipped forward with the undulations of a kris, the smooth body bent like a hilt of precious wood that thrusts the blade. . . .

* * * * *

As we were crossing the river I had imprudently asked Wootton to stay and dine, which I now regretted. But for him I should have gone straight to Rolain. But it is none so easy to get rid of a Controller of Labour. He was in good form, and told me many stories about native labourers to which I did not listen. I laughed when I saw him laugh, but I only thought of hurrying on the dinner. There had been something in Smail's attitude that now struck me as strange. His hesitation, his too fluent explanations, his haste to get away. . . . No, it had not been the candid little Smail that I had always known. This was another Smail, uneasy, evasive. But I did not analyse my impression. It was merely there, beneath the surface, a faint haunting disquiet, and a moment's reflection soon dispelled my fears. Smail must have been intimidated by Wootton; there was nothing surprising in his having been given a holiday since Pa Daoud could take his place, and if he had gone without notice I could soon find out. When Wootton had at last grown tired of my silences and taken himself off, I did no more than tell Ngah to go up early to the House of Palms, and went to bed.

Next morning when I got back after muster Ngah confirmed that Smail had indeed been given leave to go and spend a few days at home. I told myself I suffered from excess of imagination, and should be careful of unfounded impressions.

It was a Saturday. I had not seen Rolain for a fortnight. When I got back from the estate in the afternoon I called Ngah.

"I am going to stay with the Tuan Rolain until tomorrow evening. You can go home. You will find Smail there."

He thanked me and went off down the hibiscus avenue that led to the main road. I called him back.

"Where are you going?"

"Home."

"But it's not that way. Smail went by the river."

"By the river?" said Ngah. "But it is not possible to go by the river; there is no way. . . ."

I felt my uneasiness come over me again.

"Go quickly, Ngah, and if Smail has not been home, you must come back at once and tell us."

Ngah threw me an agonised look.

"I am afraid, Tuan."

"Nonsense; afraid of what? Don't say that. There's no reason for being afraid. . . ."

And as I saw that dusk was falling and I wanted to be with Rolain before dark, I left him there on the road without more words, and turned into the jungle.

"He is afraid," I said to myself, as I climbed the steep path. "Afraid? Afraid? Why? Has he any suspicion? . . . The same vague uneasiness came over us both at the same time. Strange. . . ."

It seemed a long way up that winding path. The darkness grew more intense. Then suddenly:

"What a fool I am! He only meant that he was afraid to come here at night. What am I thinking about? Rolain will laugh at me. . . ." Rolain was alone. Pa Daoud? Gone to the village. He had wanted to enquire after Smail; said he was anxious.

"What? He too?"

"He too?" repeated Rolain. "How do you mean?"

With some confusion I told him of my vague imaginings. But he listened without a smile or a word, and looked perplexed.

"Smail told me a lie," he said finally. "I didn't want to let him go. He has never been the same after his illness, and perhaps even some time before. Who knows what is going on in these Malay's souls? . . . What can Pa Daoud be doing? he ought to be back by now . . ."

"But what are you afraid of?"

"I don't know. Anything is possible."

He strode nervously up and down the room.

"We can't wait all night like this. Come along; let us go down again. We must do something."

We went out on to the veranda.

"Listen. . . !"

A sound of voices in the jungle; then lights glimmering through the branches. A troop of men appeared with torches. It was Ngah, with my water carrier and some coolies from the factory.

"Hurry!" cried Rolain. "Where is Smail?"

"He has not been seen at home," said Ngah. "But I know where he is."

"Where?"

"At Kampong Nyor."

Why hadn't I thought of that? It was perfectly simple. Smail had gone to see the little green coconut again.

"That girl? He loved her, I suppose?"

"Oh no," said Ngah; "he did not love her. He was just content to look at her. He knew quite well that she was not for him. How can the child of the sparrow fly with the child of the great hornbill?"

"Then I don't understand."

"Oh, let him speak," broke in Rolain.

"He was not pleased," Ngah continued, "when he had finished singing, and Rajah Long sent away his daughter. But that is nothing. In the morning he had forgotten it. But just as we were going to take the motor on the next day, you went into Rajah Long's house, you sat on the veranda, you talked, and then Rajah Long upset the pot of betel. . . ."

Absurd details! I wondered how Rolain could listen patiently to all this rubbish.

"Then, Tuan, Smail certainly thought—I saw it in his eyes—that the Tuan had spoken of him to Rajah Long for his daughter, and that Rajah Long had upset the pot of betel on purpose, as a man might do when he wants to convey a refusal. Then he had shame in his liver. . . ."

"Oh the touchiness of these Malays!" groaned Rolain. And they're so infernally modest where their feelings are concerned. Why didn't he talk to me about it instead of brooding over his trouble? When a man broods on things like that, they get out of proportion. And couldn't you have said anything, Ngah, you little fool? . . . They're even more reserved about others than about themselves. . . ."

As he spoke, we had gone back into the house. The Tamils were still waiting outside with their torches.

"After all," I said; "is there anything to be alarmed about? What can he do? Propose again? Carry off the girl?"

"Whatever he does it will be foolish," answered Rolain. "We must go and get him back at once. . . . If only it isn't too late! . . ."

Suddenly Ngah, who had been looking about the room, ran up to us. He was very pale.

"Tuan . . . Where is the kris?"

Rolain leapt forward and flung everything aside. The kris of the famous Panglima Prang Semaun, the kris that thirsts for blood, which Smail hardly dared to touch, was no longer there.

"Smail has taken the kris! . . ."

IV

Hendak puchok puchoklah jering
jering ta-biasa puchok di-dahan

Hendak kukok kukoklah biring
biring ta-biasa kalah di-medan

Oracles, dreams, premonitions, and even the vague apprehensions that scarce touch the consciousness, vex the soul more deeply than imminent disaster. Thus the heroes of ancient legend, already aware of their destiny, grope their way towards it blindly, but without misgiving. As it unrolls before their eyes, they cease to believe in its fatality. All who were killed in the war, knew the fear of death, and yet there was not one but felt he would survive. Only the risk of a wound was not discounted. Man loves the dreadful thrill of mystery, but he cries aloud for miracles and puts his faith in the absurd.

We imagine the persons and spectators of a tragedy as stricken and staring, because, in their set horror, they see it through a sort of cloud. That is only true of drunkards. The tragedy, when it happens, does not seem strange but strangely real, with its details pre-arranged, and seen in slow motion. If a man stands frozen in that moment, it is not that his mind is clouded; but the sense of fatality has awakened, and controls it. But with those who find the strength to act, the deed they do appears, not as the result of choice, but of an external and imperious behest. The deed, as Rolain had said, that carried certainty . . . But could I guess what his would be at the fated hour?

As our uneasiness grew, we found ourselves more and more resolved to hope. We felt spurred to action, and to fight is to believe in victory. The kris had disappeared; we must start at once. So we started in the car while it was still dark, and with head-lights that would not work; we climbed the mountains at top speed, guessing the turns in the road by the ribbon of stars that unwound above our heads between the black ramparts of the jungle. It was daylight when we reached the rest-house at the top of the pass. There we met a police inspector who had just arrived by motor-bicycle, and was doubtless also on his way to Kampong Nyor. He must not get there before we did. I slipped out surreptitiously and emptied his petrol tank. Meanwhile Rolain tried to get some news out of him.

"Are you going to Kampong Nyor?"

As the other hesitated, he went on:

"More trouble among the Malays, eh? And they say these people are soft . . . Yes, soft—as dynamite."

"What," cried the policeman. "How do you know about it? Ah, I see, you've just come that way. Then perhaps you can tell me whether the Rajah has died of his wounds."

"No," replied Rolain; "he was still alive . . . ."

Little by little, by the questions he was asked, Rolain was able to put the whole story together: a telegram had been received from Kampong Nyor at Kuala Paya to the effect that Rajah Long had been seriously wounded by an unknown Malay, and that the assailant had fled to the jungle. . . .

"Whether the Rajah dies or not," the policeman confided to us, "is not a matter of much interest in itself. But it's important for me. You see, whether a man has been killed or not, the *amok* will have to be finished off, for the sake of example. But with our legal fellows,—magistrates, lawyers, and so on, you never know what's going to happen; a pack of soft-hearted old women. . . . Of course the brute ought to be hanged; and he certainly will be hanged if he's killed his man. So if he has, I shall take him alive. But if he hasn't, I shall kill him. Self-defence, of course. . . ."

Then he explained that to take a man alive, wooden forks, with long handles, are used to grip and push him against a tree or a wall. Then he may brandish his kris and grind his teeth to his heart's content. He is helpless.

* * * * *

Amok! . . .

Amok was the war-cry of the Malay pirates of old days, as they boarded a spice-laden Batavian galliot along the coasts. Now there are no longer any pirates, but that cry still rouses a panic. In the depths of an isolated kampong, in the street of a great city, on the deck of one of the white passenger boats of the Straits Steamship Company, there is a sudden uproar. Always, it would seem, without motive. Some quiet individual, who has been eating a bowl of rice, or even dozing on his mat, suddenly leaps up and stabs another man. Then the cry: "*Amok!*": and frantic flight. For all know that as soon as the *amok* has seen blood flow, he will spare no one, neither friends, nor children, nor kinsmen. They all know too that the force within him is supernatural. It passes for a devil: but perhaps it is only despair, and the desire of death, brooding at the bottom of his heart. But stronger than even that desire, is the ecstasy of mortal combat, a defiance flung at all humanity. One against all, and he the attacker. And before he dies, he must kill once more, all his ultimate strength must be exhausted in this savage, thrilling, delicious sport. . . .

Smail, I said to myself, can it be possible?

That shy lad, so fond of poetry. What ancient instinct, smothered for centuries, could have suddenly awakened in the depths of his little dark soul? We knew already that he was *latah*, —another curious affection peculiar to the Malay race. In the course of our voyage down the river, our boatmen had soon noticed and played upon Smail's extreme sensibility. It was enough for one of them to utter an unexpected shout, or suddenly clap his hands, for Smail to fall into a sort of trance that expressed itself in unconscious mimicry. Then he repeated all the words and gestures of the man who had thus taken possession of him. One day, one of the men had cried "Buaya!" (crocodile) clapping him on the back and pointing at the river, and then pretending to dive in; and Smail had dived, clambering furiously into the boat again, only to dive in once more when the pantomime was repeated. The laughter had caught Rolain's ear, and he had forbidden any further indulgence in this sport. But it was noteworthy that Smail never lost his self-control in any real danger. It was, apparently, only when he felt he was entering the realm of absurdity that the control of his reason left him, and then he fell a prey to the most fantastic suggestions. It almost seemed as though he went defenceless as soon as he realised, after the first shock of surprise, that he was being fooled.

This frenzy that is called *amok* may well be a revenge, a self-liberation through revolt; a soul too sensitive to suggestion, humiliated by its own conscious enslavement, at last turns in upon itself, and accumulates so much energy that only the faintest pretext is needed to release it. What follows is not madness, it is a lucid frenzy that can utilise all the resources of guile. Smail had laid his plan. It was not by chance that he went off just in time to catch the weekly autocar to Kampong Nyor. He had chosen his victim: Rajah Long. And now he was prowling in the jungle near the village, alert and insatiate, like a tiger that has tasted human flesh.

Scarcely had we reached Kampong Nyor than we set out to explore the outskirts of the jungle. It was a strip of ground recently cleared, strewn with charred wreckage on a carpet of damp ashes, through which tufts of *lalang* had sprouted up. We looked for clues in the ashes.

We understood each other though we did not speak: so long as Smail was not certain he had killed, we liked to hope that he would be amenable. Wandering in the jungle since the day before, without food, beset by savage beasts, and by devils that, for him, were fiercer than the beasts. . . . Weary, sobered, he was perhaps vaguely longing for someone to come to his rescue. However, whether he liked it or not, he must be taken away. Then we would consider. He should disappear. The jungle is boundless. . . .

"I think he went in there," said Ngah suddenly, and pointed to footprints on the softened soil.

We followed the trail up to the edge of the forest, but it there lost itself in a swamp. Ngah assured us that he could follow it still further; and he was very likely right. Clues that would escape our eyes, a torn palm frond, the colour of the mud, bubbles on the surface of the water, would be enough to guide him. But how could we get near Smail without his getting wind of our approach? The three of us would make too much noise, and he would find it easy to escape. If he still had the desire to kill he would strike at his own time, but he would not choose us as victims so long as we did not cross his vengeance. Yesterday, having stabbed Rajah Long on his veranda, he got into the house, and hunted out the women; but they barricaded themselves against him, night fell, and he withdrew. But he would come back; and I told myself that he was only waiting to find out whether he had killed his man. . . .

"Listen," I said; "Ngah must go alone. Either Smail will follow him of his own free will, or he will pursue him. In any case Ngah will bring him over in our direction, and then. . . ."

"Look at Ngah," Rolain broke in; "do you think him equal to the job?"

The poor youth was livid, but his pride revolted.

"My Tuan knows better than I what must be done," he murmured in a toneless voice; "I will go."

He went, and we were left alone in the expectant silence. I was seized with awful remorse; and I wanted to call him back.

"Ah, Rolain, I hadn't the right to do that. . . ."

Rolain started, as though he had been shaken from a dream. He looked at me and in his eyes was affection and encouragement.

"I have seen such predicaments in the war," he answered. "The best soldier, the one the officer likes and would gladly spare, is just the man he chooses for a dangerous patrol because he is the fittest. One acts and the other waits. Tell me which part you would choose, and which calls for most courage. . . ."

Perhaps, in fact, I am lacking in courage. I can be composed and even bold in action, but I am weak in the moments that precede it, when all is in suspense. What alarms me is not the menace but the uncertainty. Mere nervous irritability, no doubt, like people who screw up their faces when a bottle of champagne is being opened; what upsets them is not the detonation itself, but their uncertainty as to the exact moment when it will take place. I thought of my first meeting with Rolain during the war, and of even more distant impressions, for there is not one event in life that has not been foreseen and experienced in childhood. A child's imagination is so rich that it exhausts all possible eventualities in advance. In spite of all we were told, we knew that play was more important than work;

the child's play is his training for manhood. Now, as in those distant days, I wanted to come out of my hiding-place, and shout: "I give up! I won't play this awful game any more. . . ."

It is in such moments that shades of character grow more distinct. Intent we were, Rolain and I, upon the same purpose, and haunted by the same anxiety; but beyond his anxiety I was aware of something else, a sort of radiance—I will not say of joy, but of an exaltation that assumed the semblance of joy. As I looked at him, lines from the Iliad came back into my mind: "A dreadful grief filled his heart, his eyes blazed like fire, and he girt on his armour. . . ."

I am not ashamed to admit that I should have been glad of the armour of Achilles. I knew the Malays' marvellous agility, their feline litheness. And I had read terrible stories of *amok*. One might as well grasp a cobra as try to capture an *amok* with one's bare hands. But our only chance of getting Smail back without a struggle was to approach him unarmed. I reminded myself of the days when I used to play Rugby football; I would dash at his legs and collar him hard. . . .

But events never shape themselves to our expectation. We were prepared for everything except to see Ngah suddenly at our backs, motionless, as though he had never left us. He was out of breath, and could not answer our questions. At last he said: "I went all round, like that,"—with a sweep of his arm.

"And Smail? Didn't you see him?"

"I saw him, Tuan. I was right over yonder, and I had lost the track, so I forgot what I was looking for. I leaned against a tree because I felt cold. Then suddenly I heard—chelup—chelup—footsteps in the mud. My blood went back and forward in my chest, I could not see, and then I saw Smail. . . ."

He stopped, with staring eyes.

"Well?" asked Rolain.

"He was coming towards me—he was tall, tall as a tree. I went a little farther off and I said: 'You know me? I am your brother, Ngah'. And he said: 'I know you, but the Panglima's kris knows you not'. He said it, just like that; and the kris was raised, and the point of it already in my heart. . . . Ah, Tuan, I longed to get back into my mother's womb. . . ."

"Anyhow," said I, "you ran away, and you ran so fast that he could not follow you. That is not what you promised to do. I thought you braver than that."

Ngah raised his brimming eyes to mine.

"Tuan," he groaned, "my liver was brave enough, but my feet would not stay. . . ."

"Let him be," broke in Rolain. "We might have expected it. Anyhow we are warned; the Panglima's kris will not spare anyone. . . ."

At that moment we heard the noise of many voices in the village, a stifled murmur of lamentation, and we understood that Rajah Long had just died. It was now useless to try and surprise Smail in the jungle. He, too, crouching in his lair, had heard, and his savage little heart rejoiced. And since for him death was now certain, he would return more bold than ever to look for other victims in that wailing crowd. Here we must await him.

"This," said Rolain, "is what we must do: we will post ourselves near Rajah Long's house, at the corner of the road, in the car, with the engine running. You will be at the wheel and you are not to move from it. I will disarm Smail and carry him into the car. Then you will start off at once. . . ."

"Hullo," said a voice above our heads.

We were passing the rest house, and there, with his elbows on the railing of the veranda, I recognised the inspector of police we had left on the mountains.

"Hullo," he said again, "what the devil are you doing here?"

We had to pretend that curiosity, the lure of an unusual adventure, had brought us back to Kampong Nyor. He replied that if we liked excitement, he would be very glad of our services. There would only be four men from the local police, two Malays and two Sikhs, and we should be very useful. But he had prepared his trap, and the *amok* would be caught like a rat.

* * * * *

When we came out of the rest-house an hour later, Rolain grinned.

"He said the man would be caught like a rat in a trap; well, he's let himself be caught easily enough."

The Englishman had not been able to resist the attraction of our cocktails. After a first refusal he had accepted one—just one. But there were two of us to fill his glass, and moreover each one of us had to stand his round,—a rite that admits of no derogation. Then came those anecdotes so dear to the heart of the Anglo-Saxon, of which the subject is always the same: what they call "glorious binges". The company extol the exploits of agreeable drunkards and then confess their own. But the narrator was always the last man to fall under the table. ("I've got a head like teak.") This leads to a drinking contest; glass for glass, no heel-taps, followed by sundry acrobatics to prove the contestants' equilibrium, and then more drinks, each man pouring out in turn. . . . I was chosen as umpire—horrified umpire. I knew those ludicrous jousts in which victor and vanquished bit the dust side by side. But Rolain cheated. As soon as he saw his adversary's eyes were set, he swallowed nothing more. Glass for glass still and face thrust into face, they shouted: "One! Two! Three! Go!" But the colourless gin trickled from the corners of his mouth, down his throat, and disappeared between his clothes and his skin.

"I never felt so grotesque," Rolain confided to me. "However, it doesn't matter. We had no choice. . . ."

Grotesque? Which of us, indeed, was the most grotesque? That ingenuous policeman, sure of his victory, boasting that drink had never kept him away from duty; opposite him the man whom I still called Rolain, but hardly recognised, with his mask of gaiety, his false laughter. . . . But in that mask there were the eyes that could not lie, and kept gazing down the long deserted road. Then the tragic element reappeared in this absurd scene. I told myself that all this was only absurd because things were happening, in some sort, in too natural a fashion. A threat hung over us. I knew it and I did not believe it. I ought to have had a sense of breathless ecstasy such as we feel when reading of other men's adventures. This drunkard's contest was an incongruity. We look for fine adventures when we risk our lives, 'but life is alway sordid. . . .

And yet what more sumptuous setting could there be for the adventure that must come? Kampong Nyor . . . The first time I thought we had arrived on a day of festival. It was yonder by the river: coconut palms, gold against a blue sky, and their shadows like blue flowers on golden sand; sarongs and nets drying in the sun, canoes of every hue—and that light-hearted folk who have the time to live, who loiter, and go fishing when the weather is fine as if they were going on a pleasure trip. . . . Here was the reverse side of the picture, less brilliant certainly, but in the glare of the late afternoon light, the red road between the blue-washed shops, the vertical signboards, the display of stuffs and fruit,—all was so clear-cut, so gay and self-assured. . . . In that moment, I accepted what was to come, as I had done in the war: so that I died under a clear blue sky, I did not care.

The sky was clear above our heads, but towards the west it was dimmed by a diffused haze in which the sun seemed to coagulate as it sank. Then, slowly, it dissolved, to be followed by one of those yellow afterglows that troubled Smail's soul. Smail would come out of the jungle, urged by the malignant *badi*. Like an echo of my thought, Rolain said: "Now he will come."

And suddenly he came, and we stood there fixed, uncomprehending. He sprang up between two houses, so fragile and so lost in that wide street, a picture to behold, running with the lissom movements of the young dancer, his little kris like a plaything in his hand. Was this an *amok*? I looked at him as I would have looked at a film-figure. A little curiosity and no emotion. I had no time to think, but a memory rose to the surface of my consciousness, the recollection of a like impression, in just such another mystery-laden silence: a thin line of men appearing suddenly on a deserted plain, men like ourselves, with their rifles under their arms, advancing,—who can tell why? One can see their features, their living, anxious, weary eyes. . . . One cannot think of them as dangerous. . . .

A cry: "Amok!" and a confusion of voices. In that apparently empty street I saw people running, dashing into shops. They all looked like automata. A tiny child was left alone, a Chinese doll clad in a sort of harlequin's vest between its shaven head and its little flat posteriors. Pitiful gnome. It toddled forward: I was fascinated: it would run into the *amok*. . . . Ah! They pass, and nothing happens . . . But a woman, who seems to have sprung from nowhere, rushes towards the child, tripping on little Chinese feet that cannot walk. . . . A shock, the lashing lunge of the cobra. . . . She falls. . . .

In the car, behind me, I heard a groan: "Tuan! Tuan!"

Rolain was standing in the middle of the road, motionless, with arms outstretched.

I knew that I ought not to move. I clutched the quivering wheel, but the vibration slipped into my nerves, swept through me like an electric current, and all my blood throbbed upwards. . . . Then suddenly something broke, the contact snapped. I let go the wheel, leapt wildly from the car, and plunged. . . .

V

Kalau tuan mudek ka-ulu
charikan sahaya bunga kemoja

Kalau tuan mati dahulu
nantikan sahaya di-pintu shurga

It was my fault, I know quite well. I ought not to have done it. I had not the courage to wait a few seconds longer, the few decisive seconds. When Rolain cried "Smail!" and Smail stopped as though petrified, and let himself be seized and carried like a child,—if I had been at my post that moment, we could have dashed off and disappeared before they intervened. But when I saw the tall Sikh leap up and fall, with a gash in his throat and beard stained with crimson, and the *amok* still moving forward with raised kris, burning eyes, and the set grin of triumph . . . I thought only of stopping him, of rescuing my unarmed friend whom he would stab while I looked on. I grabbed his legs, but he stepped aside and I felt a violent blow upon my shoulder, a blow that made me dizzy. . . . The rest was like the vision of a dream when eyes and brain alone are active, and the limbs are inert and will not obey. I saw Rolain grip Smail, drag him away and hoist him into the car; then that diabolic English policeman rushing from the rest house, rallying his men, the wrenching struggle over the body, Rolain gradually weakening, his haggard eyes on me in a silent desperate appeal. Then, at last, I leapt, but too late: Rolain tottered and had nearly let go. . . . And suddenly the kris in his hand rose, dripping blood, and plunged to the hilt into the shoulders of Smail. . . . I saw the back bend and the head droop, and they all fell in a heap upon the corpse.

In a moment they were on their feet, the policeman cried: "Murder! Murder! Arrest him!" But I pushed Rolain into the car,—and the car forged ahead through the crowd. . . .

At this point my memory becomes clouded. I was no more than a mechanism with the spring wound up. If I found the strength to act, that was merely because it had been foreseen that all this would end in flight. My limbs did not obey my empty brain, but a reflex force that kept them tense. I fled like an animal wounded to death, like a beheaded duck that walks on until it drops. A panic impulse, without goal or purpose. The contraction of my muscles, the vibration of the car, and the wind, stifled the tumult in my heart.

I watched the road speed towards us, and vanish under the bonnet like a red torrent. This was my first conscious impression: a great jet of blood that must be absorbed and quenched. I felt soaked in it already. There was a viscous substance on my sleeve and on my chest, and my clothes were sticking to my skin. Then, on that same side of me, as though that oozing stain had spread from it, I felt a presence. . . .

I would not think. I temporised with life. I forced myself to stay in that emotional chaos in which pain is in suspense and is not yet embodied. And yet, in the depths of me, I was becoming dimly aware that this prostrate wreck of a man, this jerking puppet, was a creature whom I had admired and loved; and I felt increasingly uneasy. Suddenly, at a turn in the road, he brushed against me, and I shrank instinctively from the contact.

And yet it was Rolain. Rolain: the name, that had just come into my mind, awakened distant echoes. As I repeated it I saw no more than the shadow of an unknown soldier in a lunar landscape. That was he, the real Rolain, though at that time I did not know the shadow's name. Afterwards it had taken shape, slowly, in my imagination. Then I had heard of a recluse who lived in the depths of the jungle, and the connection was made. I had wanted to know the Unknown. He did not answer my letters, and that silence increased his prestige. At last I was able to reach him; to reach him but to never to fathom him. I knew no more of him than the stimulus or the consolation that the contact of his mind brought to mine. That had been enough. The light that was in his eyes had laid a spell on me.

One day I saw a mask on that face. But the real mask—I fancied I saw it now for the first time, now, when it had fallen? . . .

I had a sensation of dizziness, of broken contact with life, a dim but inexorable impression that does not deceive, such as might be the feelings of a plant torn up by the roots.

In the luminous circle ahead, objects no longer rushed straight at us, but slantwise, tipping and spinning now in one direction, then in the other: high walls that rose and swerved, chill tunnels, black abysses. With one hand clenched to a burning wheel, the other insensible and frozen by a numbness that crept up to the shoulder, I struggled. I stiffened all the strength in my stiff limbs. Yet why all this agony of effort? Surely it were better to let this great whirlpool carry me away.

Suddenly the dark masses that encompassed us, opened out. I saw a gaping chasm: I was weak and unsteady. I shut my eyes. . . . A crash, a sharp stop: then silence, and darkness. . . .

A voice: "Did you do it on purpose?" I could not answer.

The voice once more: "Ah! You are wounded. . . ."

Was I merely wounded? They lifted me up and felt me. I came back to life with the deep impression of well-being, confidence, and gratitude of those who know they are rescued in their extremity, were it but at the hands of a careless foe. There is a voluptuous charm in utter powerlessness, in the abdication of the will, familiar to sick people and children, which is, no doubt, the ideal of mystics. When the vibration started again, I felt myself spirited away by a force as pitiless as a storm. It seemed that I was circling upwards in endless spirals, to the interstellar regions whence terrestrial affairs appear insignificant. Already nothing seemed to matter. A sort of lucidity came back to me, but on a higher plane, where everything grows insubstantial, where pleasure and pain, indifferent in themselves and retaining only an aesthetic value, like black and white, like the contrast of light and shadow, are gradually sublimated and purged of their sensuous element; pure paradoxes, diversions of the mind. I found myself thinking that this must be God's vision of the universe. Was I dying? It was certainly pleasant to die. . . . And yet not pleasant in the ordinary sense of the term: rather like the abstract satisfaction given by a solved equation.

Thus disembodied, I floated for a while, in a faint intoxication like that of hashish, in which thoughts become so tenuous and divergent, that they elude pursuit. Every embryo idea disintegrates before it can be grasped. One feels extremely subtle, but incapable of formulating the intellectual marvels that dazzle the mind, because, even if a word were adequate, that word would be too long: the idea has perished in the utterance and the mind is intent upon its countless implications.

My hashish was doubtless want of food and loss of blood, for I was abruptly dragged from a blissful coma in which my ideas had melted into waves of music—a music that I might well have thought was a creation of my mind, were it not that I could not control it. We had reached the top of the pass, Rolain had awakened the caretaker of the rest house, I was beset by voices that seemed discordant and too human, and made to drink a cup of scalding coffee. Then, again, the vibration, the plunging swerves. But I had regained my self-control, and my desire to live.

I now understood the tragedy of that race through the night. Where were we going? To Bukit Sampah, no doubt. Dashing straight back to our lair like beasts that know no cunning. And afterwards? Must we take to flight again? Far better to have stayed in the deep ravine into which I had nearly tipped the car. Arrest, enquiry, and a trial, and all that they involved, were out of the question. Rolain would never endure it all. Explain? Is explanation ever possible? Besides it is wearisome, humiliating, futile. The worst disasters would be better than such tedium! . . .

Suddenly I recalled my bungalow at Bukit Sampah, in its commanding position over the river and the road. There had been a fort there, it was said, a Malay Rajah's fort, in the days when the Dutch were occupying Kuala Sanggor at the mouth of the river. A nest of pirates that they had never been able to reduce. Among the undergrowth on the bank I had one day found a rusty cannon ball. From the vantage of my veranda, I sometimes used to amuse myself by shooting at some great gaping crocodile lying full length on the slime. A sorry sport since all the risk fell to the crocodile. One should have lived in the time of the old Rajah. I often thought of it. A real old fashioned siege. . . . The war, as I had known it, was nothing but subjection. Mere danger, and nothing to give it a savour, not even hatred. Oh, to revolt for once against power, against everything organised and imposing, against civilisation and morality! Like Smail. That would be fine, exhilarating. . . .

I felt my shoulder,—it was barely painful. There was only a small gash with slightly swollen edges. I could bend my arm and raise it. I grew ashamed to pose as a wounded man. Ngah, crouched at my side, kept bending over me, raising my head, and gently dabbing at the wound with a moistened handkerchief. I pushed him aside, clambered over the front seat, and sat down beside Rolain.

"Look here, Rolain, this is what we must do. . . ."

I did not doubt of his approval, and as I spoke, I realised that I might save myself the trouble of suggesting a plan which must certainly be his: for if I conceived it as the only means of avoiding the annoyances of justice, he, the murderer, was not likely to look for any other solution. Such an issue was not merely necessary, it conformed to what I thought might be expected from Rolain,—something extreme in the way of action or indifference, self-sacrifice or revolt. He had acted deliberately, if indeed under the pressure of circumstances, and would not disavow what he had done. I now found justification for a deed which I at first had loathed. And what Rolain had wished to spare Smail, he would surely spare himself. Death to escape humiliation, or merely to be rid of needless argument, was no great matter, since the commonest fate of men is to die for nothing. Had he not himself said that we cling to our life from habit, just as a dog grows to love his kennel? Yes, I thought, and there are many people leading dogs' lives whom we should think much more of if they became rabid . . .

Rolain listened, and from time to time he answered: "Yes, yes". But he said it too often and too indifferently to convince me, and I had an uneasy impression that Rolain was hesitating, trying to temporise. And meanwhile the need of action, that had sustained me hitherto, was wearing thin. I had not yet given up, but the idea that fate is stronger than the human will, was stabbing its way into my mind, and I felt a shock of giddiness—the faint quiver of the top that knows it is no longer spinning fast enough . . . I tried to stir myself, but the impulse of a plan is lost in its explanation. Possibly a few persuasive words would have sufficed. But I was now aware of the weakness of a pre-concerted scheme, a weakness due not so much to the exposure of its deficiencies, as to the fact that it gradually loses its attraction.

"Don't torment yourself," said Rolain at last; "things always work out all right in the end."

Such optimism at such a pass from a man who had just killed a man—and that man a friend—took me aback. I did not understand that in listening to me, Rolain, restored to reality by my eagerness, thought at that moment only of me, of what might happen to me,—of the need of breaking the tie that bound our destinies. I don't know what he would have done if I had said nothing. But if I then felt in him one of those mysterious withdrawals that so froze me, doubtless it was because he already wondered how he might disappear, and disappear in such a manner that I could never find him out.

A vast lassitude came over me, and I finally fell into a doze. I was in a state of strange torpor, like a child dragged from its slumber at midnight and walking with leaden limbs, that on our arrival at Bukit Sampah, I let myself be guided to my bed. I fell down on to it. I heard the clink of bottles in the cupboard that served me as a medicine chest. My shoulder was washed and bandaged.

"Tuan," said someone, "is my Tuan going to die?"

"Die? Not a bit of it. Look, it's a slight wound. He is only weak from loss of blood. . . ."

Suddenly, from the depths of the night, arose an unexpected sound, insistent and familiar. It thrilled my nerves and caught at my heart like a steamer's siren. I thought I was waking from a long nightmare. It was the sound of the horn that awakens the women to cook the rice. They were bustling about yonder, around the coolie lines. It was time to get up. The day was at hand. The day . . .

A shudder went through me. That day must not come. I must silence that call to life. I would not begin again . . .

I called to Rolain. He came softly up to me and sat down on the edge of my bed.

"Rolain, what will you do? What will you do?"

He did not answer at once. His hand was on my forehead, his gaze gathered up my own. When he saw that I was a little calmer, he began to speak. He said:

"Don't be uneasy about me. Did you worry over what would become of me when I left you, years ago, in your shell-hole? Every man to his post. One must not try to lengthen what is coming to its end. . . . A few hours then, a few months now. . . . Another time, perhaps —perhaps. . . . But it does not matter, don't you see? To part is nothing when we do not really lose each other. You must not try to find me. . . ."

I felt that what he said was desperate and not to be endured, and yet it soothed me. My will was caught and held by his, and I knew that I was now powerless. And as in the trenches he had talked to me of Malaya, here he talked to me of other things. Other things. . . . But I hardly understood him. He seemed to be leading me across space, or time, or nothingness, or life, in a light so blazing that I could not see. . . . Then I shut my eyes. No more is left than an insistent voice close to me that passes gradually into a far-off voice within me, saying: "Now you sleep . . . sleep . . . sleep. . . ."

THE END

FIRST READ BY DR.
HARGIS WESTERFIELD,
AUGUST, 1979, WHILE
WRITING HISTORY
ON THE PHILIPPINE MALAYS
(MUROS) OF THE SULU
ARCHIPELAGOE.